I0714513

EXECUTION

LISA RYAN CAMPBELL

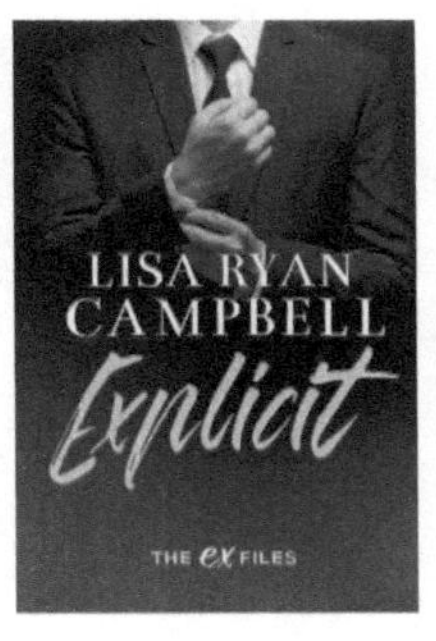

When you have a one-night stand with your next-door neighbor, and he turns out to be your boss.

Click here for your free copy of EXPLICIT!

I wrote The Ex Files series in a way in which the books could be read in no particular order. I wanted a new reader to be able to pick up any of the books and just start reading without any confusion.

This book is the exception.

Execution picks up where *Exposed* left off, and it makes a lot of references to that book. More importantly, if you haven't read *Exposed*, *Execution* will spoil it for you. So I highly, *highly* suggest if you have not read *Exposed*, please read that first. But if you have read it, well then, let's get on with the story.

Thank you for your support and enjoy.

Lisa

CHAPTER ONE

I sat on the bare mattress of the king-sized bed with only a dimly lit lamp on the nightstand beside me and looked around the boxed-up bedroom. I didn't feel any nostalgia or remorse, but was in fact glad to be leaving. It was a gorgeous mansion, but I missed my bedroom at my dad's home in Georgia. Terrence would no doubt fight the leave of absence my dad put him on, but I would make sure he didn't win that fight, because there was no way I was coming back to California. I never wanted to be here in the first place, and I was done playing my husband's tagalong. He was coming back to Atlanta with me, and from there, we could wait for this whole thing with the CBI to blow over. I couldn't get a straight answer out of either my dad or Terrence as to what it was all about, but as far as I knew, they hadn't restricted Terrence from traveling, so I packed a bag for him, had the staff box up the rest of his things, and called the leasing agent to tell him we were leaving. We were headed straight for the airport from here as soon as Terrence got home.

My cell phone buzzed from the dresser, and I got up and

checked it to see that it was once again my dad texting and offering to send his driver to pick me up. I tucked the phone into the back pocket of my designer skinny jeans without responding. I wasn't leaving here without my husband, and telling my dad that would only result in him calling to lecture me about what a big mistake I was making by continuing to invest all my hopes and dreams in a man who never loved me. I also didn't want to hear that tiny voice in the back of my head telling me my dad was absolutely right. I thought back to earlier that afternoon and the conversation I'd had with Terrence.

"Were you ever in love with me?" he asked.

He followed me out of the living room, and I paused just as one stiletto heel touched the first step of the staircase and turned around slowly.

"Why would you ask me that?"

He shrugged one shoulder. "Sometimes I wonder if I'm just a do-over for you. Maybe even a consolation prize." He took a few steps toward me until he was right beside me on the staircase. "Was there someone else? Someone you really wanted? Someone who maybe wasn't as easily tempted by you, your father, and the promises of"—he paused and waved his glass of whiskey around the opulent mansion— "all of this."

"We all have a past, don't we?" I said, and then tossed his words back at him. "Did you ever love me?"

Terrence sighed and I immediately regretted asking him that, because I really didn't want to hear his answer, even though I knew what it was before he said a word.

"Truthfully, Devon, I love the life you gave me."

Tears stung the backs of my eyes, but rather than let them fall, I remained my usual composed and dignified self, just the way my father taught me.

"That's what I thought. Well, if you want to keep it, be on that plane at nine-thirty."

He had no idea how close to the truth he'd been. I'd already given my heart to one man, and that had ended in disaster. I wasn't making that same mistake with Terrence. I just wanted a husband, a companion and someone to lead the company when my dad could no longer do it. The truth is my marriage was never about love because I'd already tried and failed miserably at it.

I began pacing the huge master bedroom while at the same time, fiddling with the charm bracelet on my right wrist. It was a gift from my parents years ago, and playing with the charms was a habit I did whenever I was nervous or worried. I stopped and glanced down at my diamond watch to see it was nearly ten minutes past eight. He'd left here an hour ago and said he would be back by now. Dammit, if he caused us to miss our flight…

I let go a heavy sigh and pulled my phone from my pocket to call him, but stopped when I heard a muffled voice coming from downstairs. Finally, Terrence was back, and it sounded like he was talking to someone. I grabbed my purse from the bureau dresser, clicked off the bedroom lamp, and made my way down the carpeted stairs. When I came to the bottom step, I wound my way through our luggage and followed the voice. It was coming from the den in the rear of the house, but as I got closer, I realized two things at once: it wasn't Terrence's voice but a woman's, and she was talking on the phone.

Was it one of the housemaids? The staff had been dismissed earlier that afternoon, so who could this be? I nearly entered, but what the woman said next had me stopping in my tracks and moving to a shadowed corner just outside of the den.

"I know what you're up to. You're trying to fuck me over, but it's not happening. I'm going to arrest that bitch Havilland, and then you're next."

What the hell? Who was this, and who was she talking to? And what was all this about arresting Hav?

"Bastard," the woman muttered.

For a moment, there was nothing but silence, and I imagined the woman disconnecting the call and impatiently waiting, just as I'd been doing upstairs. But who was she waiting for? It couldn't be my father because he was at San Francisco International waiting for me. Terrence, maybe?

Suddenly, a noise sounded somewhere off past the dining room. I looked in that direction, my eyes straining to see in the dark, but I stayed hidden in the corner of the hall. I had the eerie feeling that something was horribly wrong with this entire situation, and it would be best for me to just stay out of sight.

"Is that you? I'm in here!" the woman called out. "I've been waiting long enough, and you'd better have the money I earned by keeping you out of prison!"

Heavy footsteps sounded on the wood floors leading from the dining area into the hall. I ducked farther back into the corner, as far as I could, but still made out two tall and very dangerous-looking men walking right past me. They were so close that I closed my eyes and prayed for the shadows to keep me hidden.

"Who the hell are you two?" the woman asked. "Where's Robert?"

I opened my eyes at the mention of my dad's name and dared to step out of the corner and peek into the den. The men were closing in on this woman, and I got my first clear look at her face. I instantly recognized her as one of the agents I met that day I visited Eric Sawyer at the CBI offices. Gone was the pleasant and carefree look she had that morning. Now, her features were laced with irritation and a trace of fear.

"I said, who are you?" she asked again, but the men didn't answer and continued to slowly advance on her.

I watched in horror as they flanked her on both sides. The woman—Maya, that was her name—started to go for the gun at her side.

But one of the men anticipated the move and kicked it out of her hand just as she got a grip on it. It flew across the den and Maya grasped her injured hand and cried out in pain.

"You son of a bitch," she sneered, and attacked the man who kicked her gun away with a stomp to his foot and a kick to his knee.

The man yelped in pain, but before she could turn and face her other attacker, the second man was already on her. He sent a backhanded slap across her face that stunned her long enough for him to wrap his large hands around her neck. She was a tall woman, but he was several inches taller and used his height to his advantage as he towered over her and squeezed. Maya kicked and scratched, but in her increasingly weakened state, her hands and legs didn't have much of an impact.

I slapped a hand across my mouth to keep from screaming. I had to do something, but what could I do? These men had managed to subdue an agent who had hand-to-hand combat and weapons training. What chance did I and my one self-defense class stand against them?

Maya's struggles began to slow, and a wheezing sound came from her mouth as her body tried one last ditch effort to get air. Suddenly, I heard the distinct sickening sound of the woman's neck being broken.

Then the man dropped her lifeless body to the floor in a crumpled heap and looked over at his partner.

"You all right?"

"Yeah," the other spat, rubbing his knee. "Goddamned cunt."

"Well, get yourself together. The other one may still be in the house. The client said she hadn't arrived at the airport yet."

"Maybe we just missed her on our way over here."

"Maybe, but if so, we'll just get her in Atlanta. We can do her the same way as this one. By the way, break the glass and damage the lock on those doors. I want it to look like a sloppy break-in, and it looks like she cut the feed to the cameras before she came in."

His partner chuckled. "Who is she, and what was she up to?"

"Who knows? She's not even supposed to be here. The client told us the house would be empty, besides Devon."

"Remind me why we're going after an heiress, when she obviously has more money than our client?" one of them asked over the sound of breaking glass.

"It's over for Robert Foxworth. He's going to prison for a long time. I was assured that if we get rid of his daughter, the client will take over everything."

"You're sure this one's on the level?"

"I haven't been disappointed yet. Now, come on. Shake that shit off and let's go find our heiress."

I kept my hand over my mouth, willing myself not to utter a single cry. I closed my eyes and breathed silently in and out, shutting my frightened tears away. This was no time to lose it. I had to get out of here. I had to get to the police. No, I had to get to the airport. My father would know what to do. He'd protect me from whomever these men were, and even more importantly, whoever had hired them.

I slowly opened my eyes just in time to see them walk by again, and I dared to step out of the shadows only far enough to see where they were going. One was heading up the stairs to check the bedrooms while the other retreated to another wing of the house.

When I was alone in the hall, I clutched my purse in my arm, slipped off my shoes, and hurried across the marble floor to the kitchen, opposite from where the man had gone. I slipped into the darkened kitchen and crossed to one of the small picture windows over the sink. I opened it, winced at the loud creaking sound it made and chanced a look behind me. Seeing no one, I quickly put my shoes back on, lifted myself onto the counter and tossed my purse out first. I began to climb out, pulling myself through the window and then terror seized me when I felt someone grab my ankles.

"Where do you think you're going, bitch?"

I screamed and kicked with everything I was worth. He was so strong and was pulling me back into the house, but I renewed my strength, gripped the window frame and kicked and kicked. One of my heels finally struck him in the face, and he instantly released me. The sound of his enraged roar gave me the motivation to propel myself through the window and tumble to the grass below.

Fear gripped my heart as I jumped to my feet, snatched my purse from the ground and ran as fast and as far away as I could, seeking shelter under the night sky.

CHAPTER TWO

I needed to get away from this neighborhood, but fear held me captive because the last thing I wanted to do was leave the security of my neighbor's hedges. I didn't know whose house this belonged to, but it didn't appear as if they were home. I just picked a random house that was a safe enough distance away from my home in case those hitmen were going door to door in search of me. The tall hedges nestled in the back of this Pacific Heights mansion felt safe enough.

But even as I stayed crouched and trembling from fear, the logical part of my brain told me I couldn't stay here forever. I needed to get to the airport. My dad would most likely be there, and together, we could get to the bottom of this.

I pulled out my cell phone and called the number of a cab company. My car had been shipped back to Atlanta earlier today, and I didn't want to use any of my credit cards for Uber charges. But I had more than enough cash in my purse to get to the airport. I gave them the address to the house I was hiding behind and then turned off my phone and waited.

Ten minutes later, I saw the headlights of a yellow cab in front of the mansion. With a deep breath, I crept from behind the hedges, looked around, and then ran to get inside the cab.

"Take me to the airport, please, and hurry."

"Yes, ma'am," the driver said, switching on the meter and pulling off.

It was early evening, but there was still a bit of traffic on the roads, so it took almost forty-five minutes to get to the airstrip for the private jets. But the cab driver was forced to slow down well before we arrived at the private plane my father had leased, and when I saw why, my heart sank.

"I don't think we can get any closer than this, ma'am."

Red and blue strobe lights lit up the night as police cars, dark SUVs, and unmarked vehicles all crowded the area.

What was going on? Where was my dad?

On instinct, I pulled my cell phone from my purse and then just looked at it. I didn't want to turn it on and use it, because if I did, whoever was looking for me would surely find me once I made a call. But I had to get in touch with my dad, and this is where he said he would be.

"Ma'am, are you all right?"

"Just give me a second," I said, and saying a quick prayer, I turned on my phone.

When the home screen came to life, I went to my missed calls and dialed my dad.

"This is Robert Foxworth. I'm not available to take your call..."

I wanted to scream. I looked out onto the airstrip, searching among the vehicles and law enforcement personnel to see if I could spot him or anyone from his team. But my eyes grew wide with shock when I spotted two men who looked all too familiar. Two tall, burly, and dangerous-looking men with badges clipped to their waists.

"Oh my God."

"Ma'am, what do you want me to do?" the cab driver asked, impatiently.

They were the men who were in my house. They'd killed Agent Landon, and it was apparent they were with law enforcement. I was so caught up in the frightening realization that it didn't even register with me when they turned, noticed the cab, and then me, staring at them—recognizing them.

"Shit!" I turned away and screamed at the cab driver. "Get out of here! Get out of here now!"

"What the hell, lady? Where do you want to go?"

"Just drive!"

I had no idea where I needed him to take me. I didn't know anything about this city, so I had no idea where a good place to hide would be. But as we got further away from the airport and the meter was quickly ticking up, I was mentally counting the cash I had left in my purse.

Twenty minutes later, I spotted a diner on a somewhat quiet and desolate street and told the driver to pull over.

"Where are we?" I asked, handing him his fare.

"Just outside Mission," he answered. "You're sure you're going to be okay? Do you want me to take you to the police station instead? I won't charge you."

"No," I rushed to say. "I don't need the police. I'll be fine. Thank you."

He looked unconvinced, and I gave him another twenty-dollar bill from my wallet, which was painful, because it was becoming quickly apparent that I was running low on funds. But it was necessary.

"That's for you. Please don't tell anyone you saw me."

He slowly took the money and nodded. I got out and headed for the light and warmth of the diner. By now, it was the late dinner hour and several customers were inside. I chose a booth at the back with a clear line of sight to the entrance and the parking lot, sat down, and peered out the window. It wasn't a bustling part of the city, which worked perfectly for me. There was even a motel across the street, and I hoped to God it was the kind that didn't ask too many questions.

"Here you go."

I looked up as a tired and overworked-looking woman with stringy brunette hair handed me an oversized plastic menu and a glass of water.

"I'll just have a coffee and club sandwich," I said, handing the menu back.

She nodded and was gone just as quick as she'd arrived. With some semblance of privacy, I dug in my purse, pulled out my cell phone and looked for any missed calls. My dad had called back, but in my attempt to get away, I must have had my phone on silent.

"Dammit," I muttered.

My thumb hovered over his name. I wanted so badly to call him back, but then my mind zoomed to the two men who were in the house. They were cops. They'd killed a state agent and had obviously been paid by someone to kill me. As cops, they had access to cell tower data and phone records and...

I looked down at my phone with regret. Surely, they'd be able to track me with my phone just being turned on. At least that's what I remembered from the movies.

Thinking quickly, I grabbed an old receipt and pen from my purse, scrolled to my directory, and wrote down as many numbers in my contacts that I could, starting with those that I trusted the most. When the back of the receipt was filled, I powered down my phone, opened up the back and took out the sim card and broke it in half, which is something else I learned from TV. I then got up, headed to the ladies' room, and smashed the phone over and over again until I could flush pieces of it down the toilet.

That was as much as I could do for the time being. By the time I came out of the restroom, my food had arrived, and I dug into the sandwich and crispy fries with abandon. I thanked my server for the hot coffee and doused it with cream and sugar as I thought about my next move.

CHAPTER THREE

s soon as Reese opened the door to his loft apartment, Emma, his black Labrador, was there to greet him.

"Hey, girl," he said, dropping his messenger bag to the ground and his mail and keys in a dish on a side table. He then knelt and rubbed behind her ears. "You ready for a walk?" he asked, grabbing her leash from the same table.

"I already walked her," a voice said, coming to stand in front of him. "She's just happy to see you."

Reese looked up and saw Teresa holding a tablet. He stood and frowned at her.

"What's going on?" he asked.

Teresa was a journalist for the *San Francisco Chronicle* and an old friend who he'd met when he'd moved to San Francisco after his divorce from Beverly was final. They'd dated briefly, then decided to just remain friends with the occasional personal touch. In truth, he believed the only reason they still slept together was because it was familiar and to keep the feelings of loneliness at bay. With careers as demanding as theirs, it wasn't easy to meet people, let alone give relationships the nurturing they needed. For now, this simple arrangement with no strings attached suited the both of them. To make things even easier, he'd given her a key to his place; however, she usually didn't show up like this without calling him first unless something was wrong.

"Have you seen the news?" she asked.

He shook his head, noticing her brown eyes were wide with excitement and the accent of her Latina heritage was much more noticeable. He took the tablet from her outstretched hand and saw she already had the news app open and a video on pause. He pushed the play icon, and his entire body stilled the moment he heard the on-site reporter speak.

"Tonight, California Bureau of Investigations agents and the SFPD are surrounding this Pacific Heights home investigating the brutal murder of CBI Agent Maya Landon. The CBI and SFPD are in search of Terrence Miller and Foxworth Pharmaceuticals heiress, Devon Foxworth-Miller for questioning..."

Reese stood frozen with shock, staring at the wedding photo of Terrence and Devon on the news screen.

"All major networks are reporting it," Teresa said.

Reese didn't say anything, but continued to listen to the news coverage while a slew of questions gathered in his mind. How did Devon—spoiled, rich, uptight, and controlling Devon Foxworth—get herself mixed up in the murder investigation of a CBI agent? And did they say she was missing?

Seeing her picture made him recall the day he saw her at his office. It had been a sucker punch to the gut to see his ex-fiancée sitting only a few feet away from him. Physically, she was close, but emotionally, they were moons apart. Then, as soon as she saw him, she ran out of there as if the place were on fire. Just like him, Devon had never expected they would see each other again. Not after the way things ended between them.

"I'm asking anyone with information about my daughter's whereabouts to please come forward."

Reese returned his attention to the news broadcast and tightened his grip on the tablet when he saw another face from his past. Robert Foxworth was pleading for the safe return of Devon.

"He thinks she's been kidnapped?"

Teresa shrugged. "He was interviewed earlier and said Devon was supposed to meet him at the airport to return to Atlanta, but she never showed." She paused. "What do you think it all means?"

Reese handed the tablet back to her and headed for the kitchen. He opened the refrigerator and grabbed a container of leftovers from the night before.

"I don't know, but it doesn't affect my plans. I'll call my contact in the morning to make sure everything's still going as scheduled. I'm getting my evidence, and Devon, missing or involved in a murder investigation, has nothing to do with it. You, on the other hand, should be out there covering this."

She rolled her eyes. "My editor doesn't assign me the good stories. That's for the veterans of the paper, which is why I'm hoping your story will get me the credit I deserve."

"Then let me get back to work," he said.

"You think she's okay?" Teresa asked.

Reese put the leftovers in the microwave, set the time for two minutes and turned back to her, trying to disguise the creeping worry he felt. "Devon's always been smart and resourceful. I'm sure she's fine."

But Teresa didn't look convinced, and truthfully, neither was he.

CHAPTER FOUR

*V*ick and Jones flipped a coin to decide which one of them was going to call the client to explain how they had their eyes on Devon Foxworth and then lost her. Jones lost the coin toss, muttered a curse, and then snatched his cell phone from his pocket. His partner, Vick, watched as he dialed the number. They waited with bated breath as the line trilled on the other end.

When the caller picked up, Jones immediately launched into a retelling of the night's events, leading all the way up to the point where they last saw Devon speeding away from the airport in a cab. He thought it best to just get all the bad news out at once, but when the other end of the line lapsed into a long and tense silence, he looked at his phone to make sure the call hadn't disconnected. The display showed the call was still in progress, however, so he looked at his partner, who gave a shrug.

Finally, the voice on the other end spoke, and to both men, it sounded very calm, only not quite calm enough to disguise its fury.

"Maybe I didn't emphasize enough how important it is

that she be found and eliminated. My contacts at the DEA tell me the deputy director is days away from arresting Robert. Once he's taken into custody, the board is going to want to name an acting CEO. I want it, and it would be a lot easier to assume the role if she weren't still living."

The rest was left unsaid, but Vick and Jones didn't need it explained to them. They knew what the plan was, and they knew why.

"This needn't be as difficult as you two are making it. She's running, and a spoiled, rich daddy's girl like her is out of her element. You have a record of her closest contacts, and pretty soon, she's going to get desperate enough to call on one of them, if she hasn't done so already."

"We're on it," Jones said, a plan already forming in his mind.

"Don't call me back until it's done."

Then the call ended.

"What do you want to do?" Vick asked.

"Let's pull up her social media accounts and see who interacts with her."

Vick shook his head as he pulled out his own phone. "A socialite like her is going to have plenty of friends. Where do you want to start?"

Jones pulled his phone out and began scrolling. "There's got to be at least one person she considers her closest friend. Someone who's not hanging around for just status and money. Let's find out who that is."

CHAPTER FIVE

"That'll be $127 for two nights, and I'll need a picture ID."

I handed the last bit of my cash to the desk clerk and searched through my wallet. Tucked in the back pocket, behind all my credit cards, was an old fake ID I had from when I was eighteen, when my friends and I wanted so badly to get into the twenty-one-and-over clubs. I'd held onto it simply for nostalgia, but at this moment, I was glad I'd done so. The picture made me look so much older than eighteen, and now at thirty-six, it would be perfect. I handed the ID over and held my breath as he scanned it.

"Ah, so you're from Georgia," he said, reading the license.

I nodded. "That's right."

"Just here for a visit?"

"Something like that," I said, and put my hand out for my key card as a silent gesture for him to hurry up.

"All right, your room is on the first floor right around the corner, and there's fresh coffee in the morning. Have a good night."

"Thanks."

I snatched the key card and my ID from him and hurried to room 111. Once there, I looked around while fumbling to slide the card into the slot. My paranoia had me convinced that someone was on my heels, and it wasn't until I got inside the room, locked the door and engaged the latch chain that I felt the tiniest smidgen of relief. I put my back to the door, leaned against it, and closed my eyes while breathing slowly in and out.

You're okay. You're okay, I chanted repeatedly in my head.

I moved to the window and peeped out the blinds to make sure no one was out there watching me and then shut the drapes and switched on the bedside lamp. I spotted the TV remote next to the TV, flipped it on, and turned up the volume on the first local news station I found. Just as I'd feared, I was the top story. God, I hoped the desk clerk didn't watch the news.

"Tonight, murder surrounds this quiet Pacific Heights neighborhood where vice-president of Foxworth Pharmaceuticals, Terrence Miller and his wife, Foxworth Pharmaceuticals heiress, Devon Foxworth-Miller, were staying while launching the new pharmaceutical plant in Bayside. Maya Landon, a decorated agent with the CBI, was found brutally murdered in the home, yet law enforcement has not been able to find the Millers."

Plastered on the screen was a wedding photo of Terrence and me, while the reporter stated that both of our whereabouts were unknown and that authorities were searching for us in connection to Agent Landon's murder.

I sat on the edge of the bed, pulling at my charm bracelet and staring numbly at the screen. I was on the run from not only hired hitmen who were also cops, but from all of law enforcement. The CBI wanted to question me about the death of one of their own, but how could I ever turn myself in now and tell them what I knew? What if those cops, moonlighting as hitmen, had connections with other law enforcement agencies? I could be talking to one of their buddies who would make me disappear in a heartbeat if I came forward to finger those men as murderers.

I thought about Havilland Sawyer. She was an agent with the California Bureau of Investigations. Even though we weren't close, and I did show up at her house unannounced to ask her what was going on between her and my husband, I was almost certain she wasn't a crooked agent. She had ethics and morals and cared about her job and the work she did. Still, if I turned myself in, I would be exposed, and just because Havilland, or even her husband Eric was trustworthy, didn't mean I could trust the people they worked with.

Where was Terrence?

Obviously, he'd never come back to the house, or if he did, I missed him in my escape. What if he had come back, found those two men, and they killed him? I shook that thought away because they would have likely left his body lying right there in the den next to Maya.

I closed my eyes but couldn't get the image or even the sound of that woman's neck being snapped out of my head. It ran over and over in my mind on a torturous loop. I then opened my eyes and looked over at the room phone. I longed to call my father. Despite our differences when it came to my marriage, he always had a way of fixing things and making everything okay. But I couldn't risk that, either. By now, whoever was after me was watching him, too, expecting me to make contact and meet him. I was quickly running out of options, and that dreadful feeling of being trapped scared the shit out of me.

CHAPTER SIX

Michaela sat patiently listening to her clients discuss the layout of the gourmet kitchen in the 4500-square-foot home they were building in Alpharetta. While they talked amongst themselves, she snuck a peek at her phone, hoping that Devon had called sometime during her meeting.

Last night, after putting the boys to bed, she and her husband James had sat in the family room, their eyes glued to the TV as news of Devon's involvement in a murder played out. Michaela had to keep re-reading the names at the bottom of the screen to convince herself that this was indeed her best friend and sorority sister currently missing and wanted for questioning in the death of a CBI agent.

"Oh my God," she said, racing to her cell phone.

"Michaela!" James called after her. "Don't panic."

She scrolled to Devon's contact information and dialed, but the call went to voice mail. She tried two more times before giving up.

"She's not answering."

"I'm sure she's fine."

"But where could she be?"

James gave a short chuckle. "She's probably hiding out somewhere on a beach in the Maldives, laughing her ass off at all this media attention."

Michaela rolled her eyes and shook her head in frustration. She wasn't sure why she expected any sympathy from him. In all the years she'd been married to him, James never had warmed up to Devon. He believed she was just like any other rich girl—spoiled and never wasting a moment to flaunt her privilege. No matter how many times Michaela had tried to convince him that her friend had a good heart, he refused to see it. It got so bad sometimes that Michaela had to tell him to back off.

So, even though she had woke up on time, got the twins off to school, and prepared the architectural plans for her client meeting, her nerves were still frayed. She wanted to tell James that if Devon had taken an impromptu vacation, she would have returned Michaela's calls and texts, or at the very least, returned her father's calls.

Something was wrong.

"Michaela?"

She focused on the couple. "Sorry. What was that?"

"Is it too late to add a wraparound deck to the back? Kelly and I want a space outdoors to entertain our friends."

"Of course."

She smiled, pulled out her phone, and added a note to update the plans. Just as she did so, a call came in from an unknown number. Usually, she would ignore it, but intuition told her to answer.

"Give me a minute, ladies," she said, holding up one finger and answering the call.

"Michaela Brown."

"Michaela, it's me."

As soon as she heard the familiar voice on the other end,

she stood from the table in surprise, toppling the chair over behind her.

"Are you all right?" Kelly asked in alarm.

"I'm fine." Michaela gathered herself and gave them a friendly smile. "You two keep looking over things and make sure it's all good. I really need to take this call."

They nodded their understanding, and she left the conference room, hurried to her office, and closed the door.

"Devon? Oh, thank God. Are you okay?"

"I'm fine."

She sounded anything *but* fine. Her voice was shaking and filled with fear.

"I saw the news. What's going on out there?"

"It's a long story, but I really can't talk about it on the phone. In fact, I don't want to be on the phone at all. Someone could be listening."

Listening? What was she talking about?

"Dev, the news said you were wanted for questioning in a murder."

"I promise, I'll explain everything, but not now. I need a huge favor from you, and I don't have anyone else to call."

"Of course. What is it?"

Michaela heard her take a deep breath on the other end before speaking.

"I need you to withdraw as much cash as you can without it drawing any attention. Then I need you to book a flight to San Francisco."

"Devon—"

"You know I'm good for it. As soon as it's safe to do so, I can get access to my accounts—"

"Honey, that's not what I meant. I don't care about that. It's just…what kind of trouble are you in?"

"Please, Michaela. I need you to just trust me and hold the questions until you get here."

Michaela sighed and then nodded, even though Devon couldn't see her. "Okay. As soon as I hang up, I'll make the arrangements. Where are you staying?"

She grabbed a notepad and pen from the end of her desk and quickly jotted down the name and address of the motel.

"I'm on my way," she promised.

Silence filled the line before she heard Devon speak again, and this time her voice was steady.

"Thank you."

Michaela hung up and stared into space for a while. She had a lot of arrangements to make: book her flight, go to the bank, reschedule her client meetings, make sure the boys were caught up on their school projects, pack and tell James…

Oh God. What was she going to tell James?

CHAPTER SEVEN

As the boss and partner of Hunter, Bennett, and Meeker, Reese made it a habit to arrive at the office early before most of the investigators. Today though, he was there early because he hadn't been able to sleep a wink after seeing Devon's picture plastered all over the news last night.

Clutching his coffee flask and hiking his messenger bag over his shoulder, he made his way down the hall to his office, but stopped when he saw one of the other partners sitting at his desk and eyeing a file with consternation.

Reese knocked on the open glass-paned door. "Morning."

"Hey, good morning." Oliver Meeker said and beckoned Reese into his office. "I saw you finished the Lipscomb job last night."

"Yeah. I emailed his assistant last night."

"Nice," Oliver said, still looking concerned.

Reese came closer, leaned over the desk, and saw the file had a picture of a very recognizable face. "He's on your radar?" he asked.

Oliver looked up from the photo. "You know him?"

"Just from the news," Reese said, the lie slipping easily from his lips.

"One of the investigators was on a case involving him. His wife wanted us to follow him. You might've seen her. Devon Foxworth-Miller. She came into the office a few weeks ago, looking for an update."

Reese nodded. "The pharmaceutical heiress. I remember. I caught a glimpse of her, but didn't she close the case?"

"She did, but before I could tell our guy, he brought me these."

He handed the folder over to Reese, who opened it and began flipping through the colored photos.

"This man Terrence is meeting with…is that who I think it is?"

Oliver nodded. "Raphael Cirillo. A known enforcer for the Lupino cartel. We also identified the woman Terrence was seen with on multiple occasions, and get this: She's a CBI agent working in the Controlled Chemical Substances division."

Reese frowned. "What do you make of it?"

"Sounds like Miller might be in the middle of a sting operation, but I can't get ahold of his wife. I saw the news last night, and it looks like they're both missing."

"And there's a dead CBI agent in their house," Reese finished.

"Jesus," Oliver said, rubbing his face. "What a mess."

"Look, there's nothing here the police don't already know," Reese said. "Sit on it for a day or two. If we don't hear from Devon—I mean Mrs. Foxworth-Miller—turn it over to the Feds and let's be done with it."

Oliver nodded, still looking uncertain. "All right."

Reese's cell phone vibrated in his pocket and he backed out of the office. "Let me know if anything changes."

Once he was away from Oliver's ears, he fished his phone

out of his pocket, checked the display, and answered immediately.

"We've got a problem," the caller said.

Reese resisted groaning aloud as he let himself inside his own office, closed the door, and sat at his desk.

"Talk to me."

"The deal's over, Reese."

He gripped his cell phone and was convinced he could crack it between his hands with the amount of restrained fury inside of him. "You're pulling out?" he asked, gritting his teeth and speaking low. "Why?"

"I'm sorry to do this to you, but I'm here in Atlanta, and you're not."

"That's the whole point," Reese said. "I needed an insider. Someone who has access to the files and could get me the information I need." He paused and tried to breathe evenly in hopes it would calm his temper. The last thing he wanted to do was alienate his one contact at Foxworth Pharmaceuticals. "If this is about what's been on the news, don't worry. Devon and her husband's legal issues have nothing to do with the company. Robert is still in charge, and that's what matters."

The man on the other end sighed heavily. "You're not hearing me. There are unmarked government vehicles parked day and night surrounding this building. The Feds are circling, and I just got an email from my boss ordering me to shred shit that's not supposed to be shredded. Do you understand? Whatever is going on is deeper than Terrence and Devon. Something is going on with the company."

Reese leaned forward in his seat and tried to keep the desperation out of his voice. "Just continue doing what you need to do. Whatever's about to go down is all the more reason I need you to continue with the plan. If the Feds get in there, I may not be able to get that evidence."

A long silence followed, and he felt foreboding in the pit of his stomach.

"Sorry, Reese, but this is too risky. Find someone else."

The line went dead and Reese stopped himself from throwing the phone against the wall. Instead, he dropped it to the desk and leaned back in his chair to think. He needed proof, but if his contact was right and the Feds were closing in, there wouldn't be any evidence left. With his skills, he'd be able to get into their computers and get whatever he needed, but that place was locked up tighter than Fort Knox. He needed someone with high-level access to give him clearance, and that's where his contact came in. Now, it appears he'd just lost that contact and needed to find another way inside.

He picked up his phone again and sent a text to Teresa.

Larkin is out. I need another way into the building. Any ideas?

It took just under a minute for her to respond.

You don't need anyone. Just flash that badge of yours.

Reese shook his head and quickly typed a reply.

I don't want to go there. Not yet.

Teresa sent another text.

What about that weird email you've been getting? Maybe that's your plan B.

Reese knew what she was talking about. For the past month, he'd been receiving anonymous emails from someone claiming to work for Foxworth Pharmaceuticals. They said they had inside information about the FDA clinical trial. They promised him the files if his firm could find Devon Foxworth and facilitate a meeting to discuss a possible merger.

He ignored the emails, convinced there was a better way to get what he needed, but still kept them saved. The sender was anonymous and the emails were always encrypted, so he had no idea if this was legit or not. Also, how did this unknown person know he was searching for the notes from the clinical trials? It had all sounded sketchy. But he was now out of options.

Swearing under his breath, he powered on his computer and sent the anonymous person an email, asking for proof of the files. Minutes later, he received a response with an attachment. He downloaded it and saw the classified document with the clinic patient name: *Bella Hunter.*

Reese's eyes widened and his heart began to speed up. They'd only sent one page, but he was certain the document was authentic. He quickly typed a reply, desperation fueling him.

Where and when do we meet?

CHAPTER EIGHT

Teresa drove in front of a small café and came to a stop. It was a popular breakfast spot for the tourists to see the cable cars traveling up and down Market Street. Normally Reese avoided the tourist hangouts in San Francisco, but he had chosen this place for a reason. He didn't know these men and wanted to meet somewhere public in order to keep things from getting too messy.

"Find a place to park if you can," he instructed her. "If not, just drive around the block a few times. I won't be long."

Without waiting for a reply, he pulled the door handle, nearly got out, but was stopped when she grabbed for his sleeve.

He turned back around to look at her. "What is it?"

"If you don't trust these men, why are you doing this?"

"Because I'm out of options."

"But you don't know who sent them, and you know nothing about the person who sent those encrypted emails. This could be some kind of trap."

"That's what I'm here to find out."

She looked over his shoulder and then back at him with worry clouding her eyes. "I'm not so sure about this."

"Do you want the story or not?"

"Of course, but not if it puts you in danger."

He sighed. "Let me just hear what they have to say. If I don't like it, I'll end the meeting and email the client that I've decided to not take the job. All right?"

She hesitated, then nodded her head and let go of his arm.

Reese winked at her and then let himself out of the car. He could see in the reflection of the glass windows of the café that she was watching him, but traffic was beginning to pile up behind her, and after the incessant honking, she had no choice but to drive away.

Reese entered the spot and maneuvered his way around patrons who were waiting for a table. He looked around the crowded space until he noticed two men sitting together in a corner booth near the kitchen. One of them was facing the entrance and the other had his back to Reese. As he made his way over to them, both turned around and eyed him from head to toe. They had obviously seen him from the street. He stopped in front of their booth and nodded at both of them.

"I'm Reese. I'm assuming you're the two I'm supposed to be meeting?"

The men appraised him some more, and then the one facing the exit slightly shifted in his seat to give Reese room to join them.

"Have a seat so we can talk. Have you had breakfast?"

"Just coffee," Reese said, waving for a server's attention. "I won't be here long. Just tell me who you're working for."

"I can't do that. Our client wishes to remain anonymous. From this point on, there will be no more emails between the two of you. You want to speak to the boss, you come through us. Once the job is done, you contact us and we'll contact the client to close the deal. Understood?"

Reese's back stiffened. "Why all the secrecy?"

The man shrugged. "The client is a high-level executive in the company who has signed multiple NDA contracts. The evidence they're offering you could get them fired, sued, and blacklisted from the industry."

"If the client is so high level, why can't they get access to the documents they need?" Reese asked.

"Because no one else has access to them except Robert Foxworth, and he's not about to aid in the takeover of his own company."

"So, you need Devon?"

The man nodded. "The client just needs to find her and arrange a meeting with her. They want to organize the board to vote 'No Confidence' in Robert because of all this bullshit he's involved in with the DEA. Once that's done, they want to put Devon in charge and talk to her about a possible merger. It's all corporate politics that has nothing to do with us. Frankly, we're just here for the money we'll get once our client gets a meeting with Devon."

Reese was convinced there was something they weren't telling him, and this was the second time someone had mentioned the Feds in connection with Foxworth Pharmaceuticals.

"What's Robert involved in?" he asked.

"That's on a need to know right now."

Reese shrugged. "Well, whatever it is, a man like Robert Foxworth will definitely have a contingency plan for any legal trouble. Has anyone looked into what that might be?"

"You ask a lot of questions."

Reese looked across the table at the second man who had finally spoken. "I like to know what I'm getting myself into."

"There's nothing more to know," he said, crossing his arms on the table and leaning forward. "Find the girl. Call us. We'll call the client. Job over. Can you get it done or not?"

* * *

Daphne was leaving work and walking through the parking garage to her car when she heard her cell phone ringing in her purse. She stopped her trek, dug the phone out, and stared at the display.

Robert, it read.

She quickly answered it and was relieved to hear his voice on the other end.

"Is everything all right?" she asked.

"No, I'm going to have to stay here for a while, and since Keith is with me, I'm counting on you to hold things down while I'm gone."

"Of course I will, but you should know that unmarked government vehicles have been parked outside this building for several days."

"That means my plan is working. They're looking at Terrence, and pretty soon, he'll be out of my life and Devon's, and I can finally put all of this behind me."

Daphne went silent.

"What is it?" Robert barked.

"I'm just worried that this is about more than just Terrence." She paused and looked around to ensure no one was listening. "Are you absolutely certain you haven't left yourself vulnerable in some way?"

"Trust me, dear. I'm protected."

"But—"

"Listen to me. I know how to cover my ass, and if Terrence even tries to name me as an accomplice, I have Keith and a slew of lawyers to make sure it all goes away. Stop worrying about it. The important thing now is to find Devon."

"I'm sure she's fine."

"Well, I'm not so sure. It's not like her to not call or check in with me, but I'm not leaving San Francisco unless she's with me."

Daphne unlocked her car, tossed her purse to the passenger seat, and got inside. Within the privacy of her car, she found the courage to ask the question that had been weighing heavily on her mind for weeks. "When you do find Devon, and I'm sure you will find her, maybe we can finally tell her."

"I can't think about that right now, Daphne."

She gripped the steering wheel hard with one hand. "I'm not some dirty little secret. Stop treating me like one. You've depended on me for so much around here for years, and now I want everyone to know. I deserve to be here just as much as she does."

"You're right," he said. "But please, let me do this in my own way. It will be done. I promise."

Daphne didn't say anything more. She'd heard this same promise before and was tired of hoping and wishing he'd finally do the right thing.

CHAPTER NINE

$\mathcal{V}$ick and Jones had been staking out San Francisco International airport for nearly twenty-four hours. Vick was keeping an eye on Robert Foxworth's private jet that had been scheduled to leave for Atlanta nearly a week ago, but he was likely delaying his departure until he found his daughter. Jones was assigned to the Delta airline arrivals gate from Atlanta.

After hours of combing through Devon Foxworth's various social media feeds, they arrived at three conclusions: She had a fetish for designer handbags, she was a foodie, and her best friend was Michaela Brown. Over half of the pictures were of Devon and Michaela taking selfies together on the beach, at brunches, and during Founders Day, where they dressed in royal blue and gold to celebrate their sorority. It struck the men as odd that Devon only had a couple of pictures of her husband. Their wedding photo got the most comments, likes and shares, but there were scarcely any other photos of them together.

"Sounds like one of those convenience marriages," Vick

surmised. "You know, the kind where they marry just for the benefits."

Jones harumphed. "After being married to Jamie for twenty years, that's what it started to feel like. That's why I left her ass."

They then moved to Michaela Brown's social media page, and although she also had a slew of pictures of her and Devon, her feed didn't have pictures of the latest Birkin or gourmet meals at a trendy restaurant. She had family vacation photos with her husband and their twin boys, photos of the boys' first day of school, and newly-constructed homes where she tagged her architectural firm. She was a wife, mom, and career woman. She led a normal life, and because of that, she was easy to track. The next thing they did was look at her bank accounts. The day before, she'd withdrawn three thousand dollars, which wasn't too odd, considering she made good money. But that same day, she'd bought a plane ticket to San Francisco with her credit card.

Jackpot.

Jones checked the picture on his phone of Michaela Brown and compared it to the faces of the arriving passengers. Exactly thirty-five minutes after the latest Delta flight from Atlanta landed, he spotted Michaela exiting the airport, wheeling her carry-on luggage behind her.

"I've got eyes on her," he said into the mic on his lapel.

"All right, stay with her," Vick radioed back. "I'll keep an eye on Foxworth's plane."

"Copy that," Jones said, and slowly trailed Michaela to the rental car center.

He winced at the pain in his kneecap that still smarted courtesy of that CBI bitch they'd taken out, but he shook it off as excitement flooded through him at the possibility of a big payday once they took care of Devon Foxworth.

Michaela was going to lead them right to her.

CHAPTER TEN

I got a call from Michaela that she would arrive around lunchtime, so I checked out of the motel this morning and waited at the diner, killing time by nursing a donut and free coffee refills paid with the change at the bottom of my purse. Michaela was my only lifeline, and if she didn't show, I didn't know what I would do next. I'd cut up and tossed all of my credit and bank cards to keep from using them. I still had my ID and passport, but without cash, I was stuck.

I picked up the spoon and stirred my coffee some more, trying to avoid the eyes of the servers, who were no doubt starting to wonder why I was there so long. But as I looked down into the swirling mocha liquid, I heard a voice that made my heart leap.

"Hey there, soror."

I looked up, and seeing my best friend's smiling face with her beautiful milk chocolate skin and stylish pixie cut was enough to snap the stress that had been building up inside of me. Tears swam in my eyes as I slowly stood. By the time she brought me into her arms, I was quietly sobbing.

"It's okay, honey," she said, holding me tightly, and then slowly pulled away to look at my face. "Let's get you out of here. You have everything?"

I held up my purse, which was my only belonging, and put some change on the table for my coffee and donut. I then followed her out of the diner to a parked rental car. Once we got inside and locked the doors, I looked around for anything or anyone suspicious, but didn't have a clue as to what I should be looking for. Finally, I turned back in my seat, laid my head back against the headrest, and released a heavy breath.

"Let's go get you some real food," she said, "and then we can talk."

I nodded, and forty minutes later, Michaela had checked me into a nicer hotel under her name and we were in the hotel restaurant having a breakfast of eggs, toast, and fruit to soak up all that coffee I'd had earlier.

"Are you sure you weren't followed?" I asked.

"As sure as I can be." She reached across the table and clutched my hands, which I only realized now were shaking.

"Tell me what's going on. You sounded so scared on the phone, and you look scared now."

I took a deep breath and retold the events of the past couple of nights. Michaela listened, her eyebrows rising with every sordid detail. By the time I finished, my plate was nearly clean and my orange juice glass empty, but Michaela had barely touched her food.

"Jesus, Devon, we need to go to the police."

"No! I told you, those men who killed that woman were cops. If I go to the police, how would I know who to trust?"

"But—"

"No, Michaela! If I come out of hiding, that will put a target on my back." I looked around the restaurant, and even though she'd given me a dark wig to cover my hair, I still felt exposed. "I want to call my dad, but I know those people are watching him like a hawk."

I put my elbows on the table and braced my fists against my forehead. Then I slammed them down on the table, causing the plates and glasses to shake.

"Dammit, I feel so lost. I don't know what to do!"

Michaela made a hushing sound. "All right, calm down. People are staring at us."

I looked around, embarrassed, as I met the curious stares of other patrons and gave a soft chuckle.

"Sorry," I said, meekly.

Michaela smiled and then snapped her fingers as an idea came to her. "Your dad would never leave San Francisco without you. We can at least drive by his hotel. Where's he staying?"

"The St. Regis."

"Let's go change your clothes first, and then we'll take a drive by there and I'll leave a message for him at the front desk."

I shook my head. "I don't know. It might not be safe."

She reached over and grasped my hand. "Dev, I'm not trying to pile on your stress, but right now, your only other option is to stay in hiding, and if these men are as good as you say they are, it will only be a matter of time before they find you. We have to *do* something."

She was right. Hiding could only go on for so long. It was time to make some bold moves, and with Michaela by my side, I was feeling a little braver.

* * *

We waited until sundown to drive to the St. Regis. I hated to turn to him, especially knowing those cops were working for someone who wanted to ensure his downfall, but Michaela was right—I was out of options, and I needed to ask my father what those men meant by him "going down." In my mind, that meant he was about to be arrested, but for what? What was he involved in, and what did it have to do with the company? I swore to myself I wouldn't let him do his usual bit of coddling or patronizing me into forgetting the whole thing and simply trusting him to handle it. I'd had enough of being kept in the dark like some fragile woman. Terrence was missing, my father and the business were being threatened, and I was being hunted.

It was past time for some straight answers.

When we came to the hotel, nestled in the heart of what was known as the SoMa district, Michaela didn't stop but drove twice around the block, ensuring there were no suspicious-looking cars or people around. We also checked for any news vans, but all seemed quiet on this street. She parked a block away, I donned my wig and baseball cap, and we made the short trek to the hotel entrance.

When we got to the lobby, she had me sit in a leather club chair in a corner while she went to the front desk. From my vantage point, I watched as the desk clerk picked up the phone and dialed my father's room. My heart leapt when I saw the clerk speaking to someone on the phone. It had to be my dad. Thank God! Soon Michaela was subtly motioning me to follow her to the bank of elevators, and I quickly caught up to her. My excitement, coupled with my relief, was too much to bear.

"What did he say?" I asked in a hushed whisper.

"It wasn't your dad," she said, regretfully. "It was his lawyer, Keith Hayward. Do you know him?"

I nodded. "He's general counsel for the company. Did he say where my dad was?"

"No. He only asked for us to come up and that he'd explain everything."

With Keith's permission, the desk clerk had given Michaela a key card that provided access to the private suites. When we got to the suite my father was staying in, Keith was standing by the open double doors and regarding me with shock.

"Devon, my God, where have you been? Are you all right?"

"It's a long story," I said as he ushered us inside the luxurious room. "But I'm fine. Where's my dad?"

"Have a seat, both of you," he said, closing the doors and engaging the latch.

He even checked the peephole for a moment, which gave me pause.

"Keith, what's going on?" I asked. "Where's my dad?"

He turned back to face me, and the look on his face erased the momentary relief I'd felt only seconds ago.

"I shouldn't be telling you this. Your father has always made it a priority to keep you separate from his business dealings, but, I'm worried, and you deserve to know the truth. He left here with his driver, Miles, an hour ago to meet your husband at Pier 96."

That shocked me. "Terrence is with Dad?"

"Yes. They had a business meeting, for lack of a better word."

"A business meeting at this time of night?" Michaela asked, her voice filled with skepticism.

He nodded. "That's as much as I can say. The point is, he should've returned by now, and I can't reach him on his cell."

Michaela looked over at me, silently asking what I wanted to do. Part of me wanted to go to Pier 96 and see what was going on myself, but that sounded like a very bad idea.

Keith came to sit beside me on the sofa. "What's happening? It's all over the news that there was a murder in your home."

"That's what I need to talk to Dad about," I said. "There's a lot going on and a lot of questions floating around that only he can answer. But the short version is that someone's trying to kill me."

Keith's eyes widened, and his dark skin grew slightly pale. "Are you sure?"

"Two men were at the house that night. They killed Maya Landon, but they were looking for me. I barely escaped, and I've been on the run ever since."

"Jesus," he groaned.

"Keith," I pressed, "they said Dad was going down, and whoever was after me would take over the business once I'm out of the way. Do you have any idea what any of this means?"

Keith hesitated, and I saw the briefest look of realization on his face, but then it was gone. He quickly rose from the sofa, and I got the feeling he was trying to put distance between us, and in essence, putting distance between me and the truth.

"I'm going to try his driver Miles this time," he said, but just as he went for his cell, the room phone rang.

I stiffened and Michaela and I looked at each other in alarm.

"It's all right," Keith said. "It may be just the front desk asking about turndown service." He picked up the receiver. "Hello?"

A pause.

"No, this is his attorney, Keith Hayward. Mr. Foxworth is out at the moment."

Another pause as the caller spoke.

"I see." Keith looked down at his watch. "It's pretty late, Detective. Couldn't this wait until morning?"

A beat passed and then Keith sighed. "Then I'll meet you downstairs in the hotel bar in just a moment."

He replaced the receiver, and I stood with trepidation.

"That was a detective with the SFPD. They're looking for you, Devon. I'll distract him in the bar while you two get away."

He handed me his card with his cell phone number and email on it. "Call me when you know anything or if you need anything."

Michaela gave him her number to do the same, and we waited in the room for five minutes before leaving and hurrying to the car to get out of there.

* * *

Vick hung up the phone and grinned at his partner.

"What did you do that for?" Jones asked.

"To break up whatever powwow they've got going on up there."

"So, now what?"

"We follow them to the hotel and we wait until they're asleep. We're finishing this tonight and won't need that contingency plan after all."

Jones peered out the window, waiting for their target to emerge, but something on the radio caught his attention. He heard the name Foxworth and turned up the volume. When he heard the newscaster's full report, he met Vick's eyes, which had now gone wide with surprise. Together they sat there listening to the radio in stunned silence.

CHAPTER ELEVEN

Reese powered down his computer feeling discouraged. Wherever Devon was, she was doing a great job at hiding. He was the owner of a private investigation firm with endless resources at his disposal, and even *he* couldn't seem to track her. Then his cell phone rang. He looked at the display and frowned when he saw a name and number he hadn't seen in months. She'd been saved in his contacts, but other than the occasional *Hi, how are you?* text, they hadn't spoken much at all.

He swiped the screen, put the phone to his ear, and spoke hesitantly. "Michaela?"

"Hi, Reese."

He leaned back in his chair and smiled at the sound of her friendly voice. "Well, this is a surprise."

"Yeah, I know. Me calling out of the blue like this is kind of weird, right?"

He chuckled, and in the next second, fear nearly choked him. "Jesus! I've been watching the news. Devon? Is she—"

"She's fine," Michaela rushed to say. "But she is the reason I'm calling."

"What's going on?"

"I saw a while back on social media that you moved out here to San Francisco after you and Beverly divorced."

"That's right."

A long pause ensued, and he had to take the phone from his ear to see if she'd disconnected.

"Michaela?"

"I'm here. It's just…God, Devon would kill me if she knew I was making this call."

"Don't worry about Devon. Just tell me what's going on."

"I'm in town and she's with me, but Reese…we really need your help."

He listened to her words, and by the end of their call, he agreed to do this one favor for her. When Michaela disconnected, he looked at the blank screen for a while, not believing this sudden turn of events and his sudden change in luck.

He left his office and went into the living room, where Teresa was sitting on the edge of the couch, her eyes on the TV, while Emma lay at her feet, her eyes glazing over with sleep.

"It turns out I won't have to find Devon," Reese said, moving to join her by the couch. "She's coming to me."

But Teresa didn't respond. She didn't react at all, because her focus was completely on what was being broadcast.

"What is it?" he asked, getting closer until he was in full view of the flat screen TV mounted to the wall. The evening news was on, of course. Ever since Devon's disappearance, he'd kept the TV tuned to the news channel, listening for any updates that would give him an idea of her whereabouts. What he saw now was breaking news, and when he heard the top headline, his entire world was rocked.

"Oh, fuck," he muttered.

* * *

Michaela ended the call with Reese and nearly left the bathroom when a text from James came through. He was more than pissed when she'd told him she was hopping a plane to help Devon, and they'd had another argument about how she constantly dropped everything to run to her friend's rescue. She was glad to see he was texting her now, which meant he'd cooled down.

Are you two okay?

She texted back.

We're both fine, but Devon's a wreck.

So, you heard?

Heard what?

She waited several minutes until her phone chimed again, and instead of a text message, he'd sent her a link to a news article. She read the first few words of the headline and suddenly couldn't catch her breath. She clicked on the story and read as much of the article as she could.

Oh my God. Devon!

Michaela tucked the phone away and snatched open the door to the bathroom. She raced into the room they shared with two double beds in hopes of distracting Devon from turning on the news. But the moment she heard the TV announcer, she knew she was too late. She came to a full stop and looked at Devon, seeing the disbelief and the anguish wash over her.

"We are here at Pier 96 with breaking news. Robert Foxworth, Founder and CEO of Foxworth Pharmaceuticals, has been shot and killed in a DEA raid. A DEA spokesperson informed us that Foxworth has been under investigation for over a year, allegedly selling and trafficking controlled chemical substances from the products his company manufactures."

After a brief pause, the news reporter continued.

"Foxworth was pronounced dead at the scene. His son-in-law and vice-president of the company, Terrence Miller, was instrumental in leading the investigation and potential arrest of Mr. Foxworth, and he is now under the protective custody of the U.S. Marshals. Meanwhile, questions surround the involvement of Robert Foxworth's daughter and heir apparent to Foxworth Pharmaceuticals, Devon Foxworth-Miller. She is wanted for questioning in the violent murder of CBI Agent, Maya Landon, but authorities have yet to locate her."

Michaela stepped forward. "Devon, I'm so sorry. I—"

"No!" Devon screamed. "No, it's not true! It can't be fucking true!"

Michaela started to reach for her, but Devon leapt up from the bed and began tearing around the room in a frenzy. She ripped the linens from the bed and tossed the pillows around, knocking over lamps and overturning the armchair. Michaela stood frozen with tears streaming down her face, watching her friend come undone. Finally, Devon stopped, collapsed onto the bed, and curled into a ball as though to shield herself from any more pain. Michaela slowly walked over to the bed, climbed in, and covered Devon with her arms, listening helplessly to her cries.

CHAPTER TWELVE

I must have cried myself to sleep, because the next thing I remembered, I was opening my eyes and staring at the window across from the double bed I was sleeping in. I felt a presence next to me. Slightly turning in the bed, I saw Michaela curled up behind me, and my love for her swelled. If she wasn't here, I would've been facing the worst moment of my life alone and afraid.

I slowly rose from the bed, careful not to wake her. Then I padded to the window seat, where I sat and brought my knees up to my chest to look out at the San Francisco skyline.

My father was dead, and I didn't get a chance to see or speak to him. Our last words to each other were something about having his driver come pick me up later to take me to the airport. Such a mundane conversation, because we took it for granted we'd see each other again.

Tears came to my eyes and I bent my head forward to sob quietly between my knees. He'd been killed in a DEA raid and if he'd survived, he would've been arrested for his trafficking and selling ingredients from the drugs we manufactured and sold.

Jesus. Cartels? Pill mills? Black market deals? The words from the news announcement were swirling through my head. My father was being remembered as a criminal, and Terrence was in witness protection to testify for my father's crimes.

I lifted my head, wiped my tears with the back of my hand, and focused on the view of the lit skyscrapers, wishing to God I could just disappear somewhere in the city. My eyes trailed from the tall buildings down to the street traffic below. It was after two in the morning, so there wasn't much to see, and the absence of activity was the only reason I was able to see the danger that stalked us. I sat up on my knees, pressed my face to the window pane, and squinted through the darkness to see two men getting out of a Crown Victoria car. To any bystander, they appeared ordinary and unsuspecting, but after having witnessed one of them snap a woman's neck and the other gripping my ankles, they weren't so easily forgettable to me.

As soon as they disappeared through the hotel entrance, I jumped up and launched toward the bed and a still-sleeping Michaela.

"Michaela! Michaela! Wake up," I said, shaking her body.

"What? What's going on?" she asked groggily.

I ran around the room, grabbing our meager belongings while at the same time tossing Michaela her clothes and shoes.

"They found us. We need to go."

"The hitmen?" she asked, still confused from sleep. "But how?"

"I don't know, and it doesn't matter. We need to get out of here. Now."

She stopped asking questions and slipped her shoes on. As soon as we had everything, I quietly opened the door, poked my head out of the room, and saw that the hallway was empty. I silently gestured toward the sign for the stairwell, and she nodded and followed behind me as we crept down the hall at a fast pace. When we got to the exit, I opened the door, and as soon as I did, I saw the two men coming up the stairs. One of them spotted me at the same time, and fast as lightning, raised his gun and fired. The bullet narrowly missed us. We screamed, turned around and ran back down the hall as fast as we could. I saw the elevator, but knew that even if it arrived on time, we'd never beat them to the garage.

"There's got to be another stairwell," Michaela said, panic and fear in her voice.

That's what I was looking for, but each long corridor looked the same, and if we went in the wrong direction, we would be trapped.

"There!" Michaela pointed down one hall that had a fire escape sign mounted in the distance. We tore off down that way, just as the two men rounded the corner and saw us.

"Stop! Police!"

Screw that. I wasn't stopping. They'd arrest us, put us in the back of their car, but we'd never make it to the police station. In a week, our bodies would be found floating in the bay.

"Run, Devon! Keep going!" Michaela screamed.

I ran with everything I had in me, my eyes on the fire escape sign as if it was a beacon. I got to the door and slammed it open with Michaela right on my heels. We raced down the stairs as the frightening sound of bullets from a silencer filled the air, striking the metal banister.

Ping! Ping! Ping!

I screamed, ducking my head, but kept going and prayed one of those bullets didn't hit us. Down and down the stairs we went as death chased us, until finally, we were at the underground garage. Michaela and I dashed to the car as she stuck the key fob out to unlock the doors. I hopped into the passenger seat, and she started the car, threw the gear into reverse, and peeled out of the space. The two men had made it to the garage and were pointing their guns directly at our car.

"Get down!" she screamed, and I ducked below the dashboard as bullets slammed into the car.

But Michaela didn't stop as she punched the gas pedal to the floor and whizzed by them at a high rate of speed. A bullet hit the rear window and glass rained down, but she didn't stop, and in seconds the car was propelling out of the garage like a rocket. We shot out into the street, barely missing another vehicle. The driver angrily blasted the horn, but Michaela paid him no mind as we sped away into the early dawn.

CHAPTER THIRTEEN

Michaela drove in and out of side streets, up steep hills and down back alleys to be sure we lost our attackers. For what seemed like the hundredth time, I checked my sideview mirror for the Crown Victoria or any vehicle that looked as if it were following us. Finally, I let go a sigh and turned back around to the front.

"I'm sure we lost them."

She nodded, also checking her rearview mirror. "Are you okay?"

"Yeah, just shaken up. You?"

"Same.

"So, what now?"

I was hesitant to ask, because I'd depended on Michaela so much more than I deserved, but I truly had no idea what to do and was ready to hang on her every word.

"We need to get you somewhere safe."

"Another hotel?"

Michaela shook her head. "No, they'll expect that, and it won't be hard to track you, again." She waited a beat. "I also need to get you away from me."

My eyes widened. "What? Why?"

"Because I believe that's how they found you in the first place. They probably looked up all your closest friends and relatives and started monitoring us. They likely tracked my credit cards, saw I'd bought a plane ticket here, and the rest was easy. They're watching all the people you know, so we need someone you don't associate with, and preferably someone already in the city."

I shrugged. "Like who?"

When she remained silent, I looked over at her. She then slowly turned to me, and from the look on her face, I could clearly read one name in her thoughts.

I shook my head vehemently. "No. No fucking way."

"He's perfect, and no one would ever guess you're staying with him."

"Out of the question."

"He even lives here in the city."

"I know! Apparently, he's working at some private investigation firm."

"How do you know that?" she asked.

"Because I went to his office and saw him."

"You did? What happened? What did he say?"

"Nothing, because you know what I did? I ran from him. Me!" I exclaimed, slapping my hand to my chest. "I ran like I had something to feel guilty about, when *he's* the one who should have run away. It's what he does best."

Silence hovered between us, but I caught so much in that silence and narrowed my eyes at her.

"What? You think I'm wrong?"

She kept her eyes on the road, avoiding my stare.

"No, of course not. It's just…"

"What?"

She came to a stop at a red light and finally turned to look at me. "It's just that neither of you are entirely innocent."

I narrowed my eyes even further, but Michaela was obviously immune to my anger because she rolled her eyes.

"Do you want me to tell you what I think, or do you want me to tell you what you want to hear?"

I wanted to take issue with that, but she was right. She wasn't the kind of friend I kept around to soothe my ego. I had plenty of other so-called friends for that. Michaela was a true friend. That ride-or-die type who would both comfort me and tell me the truth, even if the truth was ugly.

"I called him last night."

I looked at her aghast.

"He's meeting us in an hour."

"Why would you do that?"

"Because you're my best friend, I love you, and I don't want to see anything happen to you. You need help. So, when he shows up, promise me you'll forget the past for just a moment and be nice."

"I heard he got married to some woman named Beverly. Surely, she's going to have a problem with him housing his ex."

"They divorced three years ago."

When I went silent, she continued to press her point. "We don't have any other options besides taking our chances with the police. We need him."

I slumped lower into my seat and tried to fight back unwanted memories as Michaela drove to the meeting spot where I would once again set eyes on Reese Hunter.

CHAPTER FOURTEEN

en years ago

"Devon, do you want to sit outside?"

I turned to answer Michaela, but for just a moment, I couldn't speak as my attention was snagged on the man standing right behind me in the Starbucks line. I looked up at him to see that he was also staring at me with a faint smile and friendly light brown eyes behind wire-rimmed glasses.

"Yeah, sure, let's do that," I called back and returned his soft smile with one of my own before facing the front of the line to endure the foreign but gleeful feeling of butterflies in my stomach.

After I gave the barista my order, I stood to the side and watched with keen interest as the tall, handsome, and bespectacled stranger gave his order. He was dressed casually for the autumn weather in dark blue jeans and a light heather-grey sweater that looked good on his broad frame. The butterflies fluttering inside of me picked up pace when he got out of line and stood beside me to wait for his order. He was an attractive, boy-next-door type with an underlying mysterious sexiness that tempted me to want to know more about him. It was also a plus that whatever cologne he was wearing had my senses singing. He had ordered a single venti latte, compared to the two drinks and Danish pastries Michaela and I ordered. So, after a short time of the two of us standing together in awkward silence while the coffee shop bustled with excitement around us, they called his order first, and I heard his name.

Reese. It was original, and I followed an urge to tell him just that.

"That's a nice name," I said, and immediately felt awkward. Oh God, maybe that was the wrong move. It sounded like I was flirting.

Then I secretly cheered when he rewarded me with a brighter smile this time, showing off his straight and even teeth. "Thanks. I like yours, too—Devon."

We kept smiling at each other like a pair of awkward teenagers, because I had no idea what else to say to him. I wasn't used to striking up a conversation with men in coffee shops. But when the barista called my name, I stepped past him, and started to grab the pastries and lattes.

"Need some help?" he asked.

"I think I'm okay."

"Which is yours?"

I arched an eyebrow and then gestured to the grande iced caramel macchiato in my left hand. Reese then put his own cup of coffee down and pulled a pen from his satchel. He took my cup out of my hands and scribbled something on it.

"I don't normally do this," he said, handing me back the cup. "But you have a beautiful smile, and I'd like to see more of you if that's all right."

I turned the cup around and saw that he'd written his name and number.

Now the butterflies were full aflutter.

CHAPTER FIFTEEN

Reese waited beside his car at a Walmart parking lot where he'd arranged to meet Devon and Michaela and thought about the lead story of last night and what would likely continue being the lead story in the coming days.

Robert Foxworth—the man who'd built a billion-dollar company from his backyard shed, the man who'd been recognized as a leader in pharmaceuticals, the man who was supposed to be his father-in-law, the man who Reese wanted to take down—was dead. He didn't know how to feel about any of it, but he did know that the effects of his death and what he'd been accused of doing would cause a ripple in Big Pharm for months and even years to come. And the woman who would likely have to answer for it all was pulling into the parking lot at this very moment.

He pushed away from the hood of his car and walked toward the two women as they exited a car that looked as if it had been through hell. He accepted a hug from Michaela and when she stepped away from him, Reese put all of his attention on Devon, who'd stayed a few feet back.

She was wearing a straight, black wig that barely reached her shoulders and a baseball cap to partially cover her face. Still, he could see that Devon Foxworth, or rather Devon Foxworth-Miller, had matured. Her head slightly lifted and even from underneath the baseball cap, he could clearly see that her dark brown eyes were assessing him. He remembered how easy it was to fall into a trance when looking into them. The orbs were so dark, they were almost black and fathomless—like deep space. It was as if she kept the whole of the universe inside of them. He noticed now those same eyes no longer had the carefree, innocent look that came from both youth and financial ease. Now they were clouded with years of joy, sadness, hope, and pain from all the experiences that came with aging. But despite all of that, time had been good to her. The natural beauty of her light brown skin that had attracted him the moment he set eyes on her had yet to fade, and he hoped it never would. And even though she'd been on the run with limited funds, the style, class and charisma she carried so effortlessly couldn't be disguised.

"Tell me what's going on," he said.

Michaela started to speak, but Reese gently touched her arm and shook his head.

"She can speak for herself," he said.

Devon's brow lifted in a hint of defiance, but then she took in a breath and quickly summarized for him everything that had happened since the night she disappeared. By the time she finished, Reese's mind was in a tailspin. It was a miracle the two women weren't hurt or even worse.

"Are you both all right?"

"We're fine," Michaela said. She seemed determined to not allow Devon to speak for too long. Considering the daggers Devon was silently throwing his way, he could see why. She obviously had a lot she wanted to say to him, but

Michaela must've reminded her that she was in a precarious situation and that she could catch more flies with honey.

"Listen, Reese. These people know who I am. Devon isn't safe with me anymore."

"You're not safe, either," he said. "If they found you here, they can find you in Atlanta."

She waved a hand at that. "Once they see Devon isn't with me anymore, I won't be a threat. But I doubt they know about you."

"Okay, here's the issue," he said, turning to Devon. "You're wanted for questioning by the CBI, SFPD, and after last night, I'm sure even the DEA would like a word."

"I didn't kill that agent," she said, her eyes slowly narrowing to angry slits.

"I didn't say you did. I just want you to understand that this is not going to be easy."

"As always, thanks for nothing," Devon said, her voice dripping with venom. She then tugged Michaela by the arm. "Let's go."

Reese chuckled with sarcasm and shook his head. "Still the same Devon. Good luck out there."

"Devon, wait a minute," Michaela said, trying to keep herself from being dragged away.

"This was a waste of time. He's not the least bit interested in helping me."

"I never said that," Reese called after her. "But no surprise, you still only hear what you want to hear."

It was crazy how the things he used to find cute and endearing about her now annoyed the shit out of him.

"Reese, hang on," Michaela said, and then resisted Devon's pull on her arm. "Devon, would you stop?"

"I said let's go."

"And go where?"

"I don't know, but I'm not going to stand here any longer begging for him to help me."

Reese stepped forward. "You don't have to beg me for anything. I'd already agreed to help you when Michaela called me last night. I just want you to understand the seriousness of it all."

"I know how serious it is," Devon said, releasing Michaela's arm and marched forward until she was within inches of him. "I just saw a woman's neck snapped a few nights ago, and if I hadn't gotten away, my body would be lying in the morgue next to hers with *my* neck broken. My dad is dead and my husband is in witness protection. To top it off, Michaela and I were nearly killed this morning—by cops! So, I don't care if the CBI, SFPD, DEA or whoever the fuck else is looking for me. I'm not talking to any of them until I find out who wants me dead. Now, am I coming with you, or are we just going to stand out here in the open and keep talking about this?"

"Devon…" Michaela started to scold her, but Reese held up a hand to stop her.

Keeping his eyes on Devon, he walked back to the passenger side of his car, opened it, and gestured for her to get inside.

"Your chariot awaits, princess."

A tense silence fell between the three of them, until finally, Devon turned back to Michaela's rental and began gathering up her things. Michaela followed to help her, but it didn't take long to unload the car because Devon didn't have much, except for a change of clothes in a plastic bag and her purse. Michaela withdrew a thick envelope he assumed was cash and pressed it into Devon's hands. The two women then hugged each other tightly for a long time. When they broke apart, Devon kissed her friend on the cheek and turned to

Reese's car without looking his way. When she climbed into the passenger seat, he closed the door and stepped toward Michaela.

"Just give her some time," she said. "She's been through a lot these last few days—things that would break anyone."

"You've been through a lot, too," he said.

"Yeah, being chased by a couple of hitmen isn't exactly my day-to-day."

They shared a smile, and then he turned serious again. "Make sure you get on a flight out of here today."

"I'm on my way to the airport now."

"I'm going to follow you until—"

"No," she said, emphatically. "Just get her somewhere safe. She's the one they're looking for."

He hesitated, and she touched his arm with reassurance. "I promise to be safe."

After a moment longer, Reese finally nodded. "You check in as soon as you touch down in Atlanta."

"I will. Thanks again for doing this. I know after the way things ended between you two that it became weird with us. It's why I didn't call much."

"Stop. You don't have to explain anything. She's your friend. I get it."

Another smile creased her lips, and she finally stepped away. "All right. I have an aggravated husband and needy children waiting for me. See you later."

Reese bobbed his head once in goodbye. Michaela then leaned over to look in the passenger window, waved, and blew a kiss to Devon. He turned just in time to see genuine happiness come over Devon's face. Damn. He was actually jealous. There was a time when he used to make her smile like that. Now it would be a cold day in hell before she showed her pearly whites for him.

He got in the car, turned the ignition, and followed behind Michaela until she reached the exit that led to the airport. He then went in the opposite direction to his home, with Devon sitting quietly and somberly beside him.

It was a short and silent drive to his loft in the Castro district. When they arrived, Reese parked and looked around the street until he was satisfied no one was watching and waiting for them. He nodded, signaling to Devon that it was okay for her to get out. She climbed out of the car, looking as if she were carrying a heavy weight on her shoulders, and Reese figured the events of the past few nights were finally hitting her. She grabbed her purse and the small plastic bag of clothes and followed him inside the three-story home and up to his residence on the third floor.

When he opened the door, Emma was right there to greet them. Devon spared her a moment's glance and then peered around the space, looking lost.

"You can have the guest room," he said, nodding to a bedroom off to the right. "It has its own private bathroom. The kitchen is obviously right there, so help yourself to anything in the fridge. If you need anything—"

"Thanks," she said, clutched her belongings tighter, and walked into the spare bedroom. Then she slammed and locked the door behind her.

Reese stared at the closed door for a moment and then shook his head. "You're welcome."

He looked down at Emma, who was looking up at him, and he knelt to rub her coat.

"Don't get me started," he said to her, and then paused in rubbing Emma's fur when he suddenly heard crying on the other side of the guest room door.

He rose to his feet and slowly walked to the closed door. He could clearly hear her sobbing now. On instinct, he brought his hand up to knock, wanting to make sure she was all right, but in the next second, he opened his fist and let his palm rest silently against the door. He listened helplessly to her cries and then regretfully retreated. She wouldn't want his comfort, and in all honesty, he didn't know how to give it to her.

C H A P T E R   S I X T E E N

*D*aphne left her condo earlier than usual in order to arrive at work on time to attend the last-minute scheduled business meeting for five-thirty in the morning. She'd alternated between feelings of sorrow and numbness after hearing the news of Robert's death. So much had to be done now that he was gone, and as his assistant, it was all falling heavily on her shoulders.

He'd promised her they'd talk to Devon when he returned from San Francisco, but now that wouldn't happen. So now she had to enact plan B, which was already underway.

She arrived at the Foxworth building, avoiding the media crowded outside. She noticed the unmarked federal vehicles still parked outside, as well as the swarm of DEA officials crowding the lobby, waving warrants. She moved past the frenzy and took the elevator to the 18th floor. Once there, she was stopped by more DEA agents telling her that Robert's office was off-limits. She turned and headed for the conference room, where the meeting was just beginning.

She quickly took a seat and saw the General Counsel Keith Hayward was on a virtual conference.

"Keith, when was the last time you spoke with Devon?" Tom Burke, one of the board members, asked.

"Last night," Keith replied. "I'm sure she's heard about his death by now. She and her friend left when a detective came to see me. She said people were trying to kill her and that it was unsafe for her to show her face."

"Someone is trying to kill her?" Tom repeated. "That's ridiculous."

"It sounded ridiculous to me, too," Keith said. "But the more she talked, the more I'm inclined to believe her."

"Why would anyone want Devon killed?" Daphne asked, frowning. Normally she didn't speak in these meetings, often relegated to be Robert's shadow to take notes for him.

"She heard the men say that if she were killed, some unknown person would be able to assume the CEO position," Keith said.

"How? Robert doesn't have any other children that I know of, and that would only leave his ex-wife, who's still listed as a board member," Tom continued. "But she hasn't been to a meeting since their divorce nearly thirty years ago."

"It doesn't have to be a family member," Keith said. "It could be another board member who believes he or she has a chance of stepping into the role."

"Regardless of all of that," Shirley Fallon, another board member said, "with the DEA getting access to our files we need to name an acting CEO before the market opens or the stock will take a dive. We also have a duty to the shareholders to let them know who's now running things that Robert is dead. We all agree to vote for you, Keith. You're the company's general counsel, you know the ins and outs of the business, and you were the closest to Robert. Will you agree to that?"

"Certainly," Keith said.

"And you, Tom, will take on as acting Vice-President and COO."

Tom nodded, and Daphne wryly thought to herself he didn't need his arm twisted. For years, Tom served on the board, hoping one day Robert promoted him to be an executive. When Robert put Devon's husband, Terrence Miller into the Vice-President position, Tom pretended to support the decision, but she could tell he was livid. Now, it seemed his moment in the spotlight had finally come.

"All right, let's get the nominating committee in on this. Keith, please let us know the moment you speak to Devon again," Shirley said.

"Will do," Keith said, and signed off.

"What a fucking disaster," Tom muttered as he and the rest of the board members rose and started to file out of the room.

"Sir," Daphne said, rising to meet him at the door. "What about the DEA and the rumors that Robert was going to be arrested for stealing and trafficking materials?"

"I'm working with the media department to issue a statement. We're hoping a new face will change the blight this has caused."

"But I heard that Mr. Foxworth and his son-in-law weren't the only ones involved. The DEA is continuing their investigation to find other accomplices."

"I'll handle the DEA. You worry about getting Robert's records in order and handing them over to Keith and me. Understood?"

"Yes, sir," she said, and narrowed her eyes at his retreating back.

CHAPTER SEVENTEEN

Reese was flipping through the channels and for once, trying to avoid the news for Devon's sake. She was still locked away in the guest room, but he wanted to respect her mourning in case she was awake and could hear the TV. At the same time, he was avoiding text messages from his new partners asking if he'd made contact with Devon, and that their client was anxious to meet with her. Although Reese was eager to get his hands on those reports from FDA trials, the sounds of Devon's cries from this morning still haunted him. She was in pain, and he didn't want to look like more of an asshole by ambushing her with corporate bullshit.

When he heard the familiar sound of the key turning in the lock, he felt relieved to have something else to distract him. He turned slightly in his seat on the couch, careful not to disturb Emma, who was laying her head on his lap. He nodded a greeting to Teresa as she entered the apartment.

"Hey," she said, loaded down with her book bag, purse, and a plastic bag with takeout containers inside.

"I was interviewing a witness in Chinatown about a

murder last week, and I wanted you to try this restaurant I found." She glided by him toward the kitchen, leaving the aromatic scent of Chinese food in her wake.

"Smells good," he said, his stomach grumbling.

He patted Emma's head and disturbed her resting spot in favor of his appetite. He got up, followed Teresa into the kitchen, and began gathering plates from the cabinet. He set a few on the counter and noticed her eyes trailing to the closed door of the guest room.

"Yeah, she's in there," he said, guessing at her thoughts. "She's been in there all day."

"Have you called the client?"

"I don't speak directly to the client, remember? Just the liaisons, and no, I've been screening their calls and texts."

"Why? They just want a meeting with her to discuss a merger or whatever. Talk to her about it and see if she'll agree. What's the problem?"

"The problem is her dad just died, and I'd like to give her a few days to grieve."

"We don't have a few days," Teresa argued, taking the Chinese food containers out of the bag. "You've seen the news. Robert Foxworth was going to be arrested if he hadn't died. The DEA and CBI have been investigating him for over a year, and the Vice-President, her husband, is in witness protection. The company is in turmoil. They're going to need to name a new CEO soon, and with her running from the law, I'm sure it won't be her. Still, she now owns the business, and when all this legal stuff is over, she may be open to selling the company, or at least her controlling shares. The client gets what they want, she gets a crapload of money, and you get your evidence."

"And you get your story," he said, munching on an egg roll.

She winked and shrugged. "Sure. Why not?"

"Yeah, well something tells me it won't be as easy as all that."

"You're the one who's making things harder than they need to be. Just turn on that charm and talk to her."

"Keep your voice down," he gritted.

A smile hiked up one corner of her lips. "What? You don't want your ex-girlfriend to know the real reason you're being so accommodating?"

Ex-fiancée, Reese wanted to say, but that would only turbocharge Teresa's curiosity, so he kept it to himself and let her have that dig.

She started to march past him, but he grabbed her by the elbow and halted her.

"Leave her alone."

"I just want to see if she's hungry."

She shrugged her arm from his hold, went to the spare bedroom, and knocked softly on the door.

"Devon? Are you awake?"

Silence.

"You don't know me, but my name's Teresa, and I'm a friend of Reese's. I heard about your father, and I'm very sorry."

Silence.

Teresa turned back to Reese, who shrugged his shoulders. "Let it go. She probably doesn't want to be around people right now."

She tried again. "I also heard you had a rough few days. I bought some Chinese food over, so if you're hungry, we would love for you to join us for dinner."

After a few more unresponsive moments, the door slowly opened and Devon emerged.

Teresa smiled. "Hi."

Devon nodded a silent greeting and stepped past her. The first thing Reese noticed was that she'd removed that ridiculous wig, and now he could see her natural dark hair, tumbling down past her shoulders as he'd remembered it. He also noticed she must've found his spare closet, because she'd changed into a pair of oversized sweats that belonged to him and a worn University of Georgia T-shirt. When she noticed him staring at her, she looked down at her attire sheepishly.

"I hope you don't mind. I don't have any pajamas."

"It's fine," he said, and forced himself to look away from her before his mind dwelled too long on thoughts of his clothes enveloping her warm and soft skin, or the anticipation of the sweet scent she'd leave behind once she discarded them in the laundry basket.

She moved around the kitchen like a ghost, robotically filling her plate with noodles and steamed vegetables. She then accepted a can of Pepsi Reese offered her with a barely audible "thank you" and took the middle barstool at the large kitchen island which also served as his dining table. Reese and Teresa moved around her as if she were a bomb, liable to go off at any minute. When their own plates were filled, they joined her at the island, taking the two seats on either side of her. They quietly ate their meals, pretending to not notice Devon had only taken a few bites and was now staring off into space and fiddling with the silver charm bracelet on her wrist. Reese was surprised to see she was still wearing it after all these years.

He put his attention back on his food and forked some rice and sweet and sour chicken into his mouth. He stopped chewing his food and turned to look at her when she broke the silence.

"I don't know what my dad wants."

She divided a look between both Reese and Teresa and clarified. "I don't know if he wants to be buried or cremated. We never talked about that. I don't know what to do with that house in Georgia. Terrence and I were living with him before we moved here to San Francisco, but this was only supposed to be temporary. With Terrence in witness protection, I don't want to stay here in California, but I also don't want to stay in that big house all by myself."

She placed her elbows on the counter and buried her head in her hands. "I don't even know what I'm going to do with the company."

He hadn't planned to touch her. He never expected to ever touch her again, but suddenly, he was leaning over and putting a gentle hand on her arm. It must've surprised her, too, because she slowly raised her head, looked down at his hand on her arm, and then lifted her eyes until they were locked on his.

He cleared his throat. "There's plenty of time to decide what you're going to do. You don't need to think about any of that. Just put it out of your mind for now."

Her expression was unreadable, but she gave a small nod, agreeing with him. He stared into her eyes, and that one moment felt like an eternity. It wasn't until Teresa cleared her throat noisily that he remembered they weren't alone. He looked over Devon's head at her, and saw she was giving him a telling look, silently urging him to bring up the meeting with the client. He returned it with a look of his own that told her to drop it.

CHAPTER EIGHTEEN

My eyes trailed Teresa as she moved about the kitchen, taking her and Reese's plates and bringing them to the sink to scrub. Once that was done, she put the leftover food away in the fridge and wiped down the countertops and island where we'd been eating. She was comfortable here, which further confirmed my original assumption. From the instant I opened the bedroom door and got a look at her long black wavy hair, flawless olive complexion and killer figure, I knew she and Reese were more than friends.

Jesus, was I really hiding out with my ex and his girlfriend? Is that why she'd cleared her throat rather loudly when Reese and I were staring at each other a bit too long?

My gaze moved from her to Reese, and to my surprise and embarrassment, his eyes were on me. Had he been watching me watch Teresa the whole time?

I left my seat on the barstool, went over to the trash, and dumped the remains of my dinner. Teresa took the empty plate from me, and I smiled weakly with thanks.

I then turned to Reese. "You mind if I turn on the news?"

"No, go ahead. But are you sure you want to hear any of that right now?"

Without responding, I made my way to the living room, sat down on the sofa next to his dog, and turned on the TV. After about an hour of watching replays of my father's death and the corruption surrounding him and the company, I vaguely noticed out of my peripheral vision that Reese and Teresa were moving towards the front door.

"It was nice to meet you, Devon," she said.

I turned to her and forced another smile. "Thank you for dinner."

She nodded and Reese escorted her out of the apartment. They stayed out in the hallway for a long time, and although my eyes were on the TV screen, my mind wandered through the many possibilities of what they could be doing out there. The nights I used to visit him, I remembered it took us a half an hour to say good night to each other. The moment I'd walk away to my car, Reese would inevitably pull me back into his arms for another kiss.

"When I say I have an early morning, I really do have an early morning," I said in a slight whine, with my arms wrapped around his neck.

"You can always stay here. Shopping, lunch, and a mani-pedi appointment can be done anytime," he teased, his hands moving slowly from my waist down to my ass.

I leaned my head to the side, guessing at his tricks. "You really think I'd get sleep with you lying beside me?"

He squinted his eyes as if in deep thought. "I can promise you a full hour's sleep. That's plenty."

The front door opened and I snapped back to the present, keeping my eyes on the TV and listening to Reese's heavy footsteps track along the wood floor until I could sense him standing behind the sofa.

"That can't be healthy," he said.

"I'm fine."

"There's nothing new to report. Your husband became an informant for the DEA. Your father was going to be arrested, but he was killed in the raid. End of story. Stop torturing yourself and turn it off."

"I'll turn it off when someone can tell me why and how."

"What do you mean?"

I tossed the remote to the side, propped one knee up on the sofa, and turned around to face him. "Why did my father go down this path in the first place, and how could he have kept something like this from me?"

"The only one who can answer that is him, and—"

"And he's dead. Yeah, I'm fully aware."

I turned back to the screen with tears once again threatening to fall. God, I was so tired of crying. I was mourning my father, while at the same time feeling so disappointed in him. I couldn't tell which tears were from sadness and which were from anger.

It was silent for a long time except for the chatter of the news anchors, and suddenly I felt a hand on my shoulder. I shot off the sofa and whirled around, startling him and his dog.

Reese held up his hands. "I'm sorry. I shouldn't have done that."

"No, it's not that. It's just…"

It's just that this was the second time tonight he'd touched me. It had been way too long since I'd felt his fingers on me, and I was not yet used to how it made me feel—which was a longing for more.

"Look, again, I'm sorry for everything you're going through. Tomorrow I can take you by my office. I have software on my computer that will let you browse the internet and find some answers without being detected."

I nodded, wrapping my arms around myself. "Thank you,

and I'm sorry for snapping at you this morning in the parking lot. I've been stressed for days."

"Forget it. But maybe you should get some rest. You've had a long day."

"You didn't have to get rid of your girlfriend on my account."

He gave me a strange look and then rubbed the back of his head.

"She's not my girlfriend. We're colleagues."

I hesitated. "Colleagues with benefits?"

"I have work to do," he said, heading toward his office and purposely ignoring my question. "See you in the morning."

He gave a short whistle and kissing sound, and then Emma popped up from her resting position and followed after him.

"I never knew you were into dogs," I called after him.

"You never asked," he said, and closed the office door.

CHAPTER NINETEEN

Reese closed out the file he'd been reading on his laptop, leaned back in his desk chair, and closed his eyes. He'd told Devon he had work to do, but truthfully, he'd just used that as an excuse to put distance between them.

After so many years apart, it was strange having to suddenly share space with her. Things had ended badly, they'd both moved on and gotten married to other people, and now, years later, they were here together. She was in his city and in his home when for so long, he believed he'd never see her again. But he *was* seeing her again. She was just in the other room, so close that it was making it difficult for him to concentrate on anything but how soft her skin was to his touch. Christ, who was he fooling? He hadn't come in here to do any work. He was hiding from her.

His cell phone chimed, and he looked at it to find he was receiving an encrypted email message. He pulled it up on his laptop and saw that the sender was anonymous. But his gut told him it was coming from the mysterious client he now worked for. Since their first email, the client never spoke to him again, but referred him to the two "liaisons," as he liked to call them.

He decrypted the message and read it:

Have you made progress in finding Devon?

He muttered an expletive and then quickly typed a reply:

She's with me, but she's being hunted. It's too risky bringing her out of hiding.

He sent the message off and within a few seconds, the client responded.

That's unacceptable. Contact my men. Tell them you have her and let's close this deal. You'll get your evidence as soon as I have her location. Agreed?

Reese started to type another response, but then something at the bottom of the screen caught his eye. It was a location tracker he'd installed to warn him of any potential hacking or someone tracking his location. The icon was flashing red.

"Shit," he said, and quickly logged off the chat. He then powered down his computer and removed the battery.

Sitting back in his chair again, he frowned at what just happened. Whoever he'd been speaking to had been tracing his location. They knew he had Devon and were determined to find her.

Who *were* these people?

CHAPTER TWENTY

Ten years ago

It was Saturday night, and Reese had invited me over to his condo for pizza and a movie. But after thirty-five minutes, we were no longer paying attention to the show, the pizza had grown cold, and Reese had his head underneath my sweater with his mouth latched onto my breasts—tempting me to break my "no sex" rule.

We'd been dating for six months now, and I was hesitant to admit to myself or him that I was completely in love. I wanted him in my life, and so I made the decision to hold off on the physical to ensure that whatever this was between us remained special. But, Jesus, the way his hands knew how to roam over my curves and the way his tongue rapidly flicked against my hard and tender nipples...I wanted this man inside me.

"Okay, stop," I said, breathless and pulling away from his embrace. "Hang on. I need to talk to you."

His hot mouth let go of one of my breasts and he lifted his head from underneath my sweater with a satisfied grin. "It doesn't sound like you want me to stop."

I really didn't, but this was important. I gently pushed him off of me, grabbed my large Birkin from the coffee table, and pulled out the magazine. I flipped through it until I came to the Tiffany's ad and pointed to the three-carat solitaire diamond engagement ring that had my mouth watering from the moment I saw it.

"Do you like it?" I asked.

"Sure, but you don't have to get me a ring," he joked.

"It's for me," I said, laughing. "You said you wanted to marry me, right?"

He groaned. "There goes my hard-on. Is this the part where I run away?"

I punched him playfully on the shoulder. "Not funny!"

He chuckled, grabbed me by the waist and pulled me toward him again. "All right, but you'll have to give me a few years to afford that."

"No need to wait, because I already bought it."

Silence fell, and I sensed something in the atmosphere change. I turned to look at him and saw he was now frowning.

"You bought it?" he asked.

"Yeah. It's on order. I pick it up next week."

"It was that serious that you couldn't wait?"

"Wait for how long? You said you wanted to marry me."

"I do, but I also wanted to get my career going. I want to be stable for us."

I let out a laugh. "I think it's safe to say I'm plenty stable enough for the both of us."

Silence reigned again and now it was my turn to frown.

"You said yourself you wouldn't be able to afford it for a few years. What do you expect me to wear at the altar?"

He shrugged. "A ring I can afford to buy you."

I laughed again. "Maybe you don't understand. I'm Robert

Foxworth's daughter. An only child and heiress to an international company."

He groaned. "I get it. You're Atlanta royalty."

"Correct, and as Atlanta royalty, everyone will be scrutinizing everything about this wedding—from my dress to the flower arrangements. No offense, honey, but I can't wear just any ring. Everything has to be spectacular."

When he didn't respond, I peered at him and made a pouty face.

"Please don't be mad. I love this ring, and does it really matter who bought it?"

"I guess not."

His eyes were focused so intently on me, and although his tone held indifference, there was something in those brown orbs that said so much. Later, I would regret not asking him to tell me what he wasn't saying.

* * *

I woke up early that next morning, rolled onto my back, and just stared at the ceiling for a while before I decided to get up and be brave enough to see if Reese was awake. I opened my bedroom door, but was met with silence. I crept past Reese's room, which was right next to mine, and paused at the slightly opened door. I swung it open and my breath caught at the sight of him, asleep, his body spread across his king-sized bed. He was wearing pajama pants, his chest was bare, and he looked so peaceful and inviting. We'd never spent the night together when we were dating or even when we got engaged, so I never had the pleasure of knowing he slept with the comforter partially covering his body, whereas I liked to sleep with my body burrowed deep under the covers. My plan was to keep things sweet between us without the distraction of sex. And for a while, it worked, except for the times we got so hot for each other and dangerously crossed the line with oral sex. But remembering his tongue lapping greedily on me was not the kind of memory I needed to be having this early in the morning.

Emma, who had been sleeping in a dog bed beside his bed, rose and padded toward me. I let her out into the living room and then reached out and quietly closed Reese's bedroom door.

I decided to distract myself by making coffee and pouring food into her dog bowl. While the coffee brewed, I crossed to one of the large picture windows and watched the night give way to the early morning. I'd lived in San Francisco long enough to grow used to the mornings when the fog would creep in and shroud the city in mystery. Then, by early afternoon, it would completely vanish as though it never existed.

I turned my back to the window and made my way to Reese's home office. On the desk was his laptop. The lid was closed and I frowned at the battery lying next to it. Desperate for information from the company, I sat down, put the battery back in, and switched the computer on. The log on screen came to life, and just as expected, it was password-protected. I looked down at Emma, who'd left her breakfast to follow me into the office and was now looking back up at me. I typed in her name.

Invalid password.

Reese had studied Business and Cybersecurity in college. More than anyone, he knew the importance of keeping a secure password, so his most likely had a mix of numbers, letters, and symbols. Even more likely, they weren't actual words at all but a mix of letters. If that was the case, I wasn't getting into his computer at all. I sat back in the chair, spun around and eyed the floor-to-ceiling bookcases behind me. He always had a book in his hand, and was one of the last people I knew to finally get an e-reader, but he still preferred the sight of hardcover books lining the shelves in his office. Along the row of books, my eyes came to a stop at a framed picture. It was him, his ex-wife, Beverly, and a little girl who was likely their daughter. I remembered stalking his social media page several years back and seeing a picture of the three of them looking so happy together. I remembered the caption, too, because it was a stab to my heart: *Me, Bev and our Honeybee.*

Biting back jealousy at the sight of the happy family I'd wanted so long for myself, I turned in the chair, leaned forward, and typed in *Honeybee*. The screen came to life. For a Cybersecurity expert, Reese still had a sentimental side. I went to the Foxworth website and logged into my company email. There was a Board of Directors meeting held yesterday and they had named Keith as acting CEO. I exhaled a sigh of relief. Even though I should've been there, I felt a sense of comfort wash over me knowing the company was still in capable hands while I was spending my days hiding out from a pair of hitmen.

I received my Bachelors in Business from Spelman College and after graduation, I moved to New York for a time while studying for my MBA at Wharton. Although I had the education, I never planned to use it. If anything had ever happened to my dad, I'd counted on Terrence to take over. That definitely couldn't happen now with him in the custody of the U.S. Marshals. Keith was a good choice.

Feeling less overwhelmed, I closed the email and browser and saw a folder on the desktop screen labeled *Foxworth Pharm*, but before I could open it, I heard movement coming from Reese's bedroom. I quickly powered down the laptop, took the battery out and made sure to leave things as I'd found them. I then went into the kitchen, with Emma trotting at my heels, and started searching the cabinets for coffee mugs when I heard Reese walk up behind me. He reached around me, and instantly, my nose indulged in his fresh scent. I closed my eyes, inhaled deeply and tried not to sigh.

He opened one cabinet, pulled out two mugs, and handed one to me.

"Thank you," I said, softly, my eyes looking everywhere but at his bare chest.

"Thank you for making coffee," he said, pouring the steaming, black liquid into his cup.

He took a sip and then sighed, looking around. "All right. Get dressed. I'm going to take Emma for a walk and when I get back, I'll shower and change and we'll head to my office. Sound good?"

"Sure," I said.

I wanted to ask him about the file with the company name on his laptop, but I didn't want him to know I'd been snooping or that I'd guessed his password.

Honeybee. Where was the little girl?

CHAPTER TWENTY-ONE

It was Saturday, so the offices were empty, which was good, considering the DEA, CBI, and SFPD were all looking for Devon. At least for now they would have privacy while she did what she needed to do. Once they arrived on the floor where his agency was housed, Reese led her to his office, sat at his desk, and powered on his computer.

"Business must be good, considering you can afford a space like this in San Francisco," Devon remarked as she looked around his office.

"We do all right," he said, being purposely vague as he typed in his password.

"So you're a partner?'

"Yeah, there's three of us, and we employ about thirty investigators."

"Do you do any of your own cases anymore?"

"Sometimes. It depends on the type of project and scope."

"So you don't bother with the spouse who wants to have their spouse followed?"

He eyed her. "No, I hand those off to my investigators."

She stepped in front of his desk. "That's why I came here, you know. That day I was here in the office. I saw you, and I know you saw me."

"I did, and I already knew why you were here. I stay up to date on all the cases that come through the business."

"So you saw my file?"

"I skimmed it."

He'd more than skimmed it. He'd took it home and memorized nearly every word of it, wanting to reacquaint himself with her if only from afar. He wanted to know what she'd been doing all these years, but that file had only told him her name, address and that she wanted her husband followed. He craved to know more about her.

"Do your partners know about us?"

"No. We did what you hired us to do, you closed the case, and we got paid. Done deal. Everything else is…"

"What?"

"Pointless."

That wasn't what he meant to say, and he could see in her eyes that she believed he thought their relationship was pointless, but that wasn't what he'd meant.

Screw it. Let her think what she wants. It didn't matter. She was a means to an end. Once she was safe, he would arrange the meeting between her and the client, get the evidence he needed, and she'd be on the first private jet back to Georgia and once again be nothing but a memory.

"You said you wanted to contact your father's lawyer."

She nodded and handed him a business card with contact information written on it. "Keith Hayward, and I guess he's *my* lawyer now. He can tell me the state of things."

He took the business card and tapped it against his fingers thoughtfully. "We don't know who's trying to kill you, Devon. It could be someone in your inner circle or someone connected to the company. Can you trust him?"

"I don't know who to trust, except Michaela, but I need answers, and I'm tired of getting them from CNN."

She folded her arms across her chest, which he remembered was something she always did when she was pouting. But what she wasn't aware of was that whenever she pulled that move, it lifted her breasts and gave him the strongest desire to lose his face in between them, like he used to do when they were dating. Instantly, an image flashed in his mind where he was pressing her against the wall of his condo with his knees bent and his head deep in between her breasts, his fingers caressing their fullness and his teeth gently latched onto one of her nipples and dampening the lace bra she wore. It only took a few short seconds of that before she was moving against him in earnest, moaning and carrying on and making them both crazy with wanting.

"All right," he said, shutting away the memory and shifting away from her lest she see his growing hard-on.

He quickly typed a message, which included his contact information, and sent off the email.

"Now what?" she asked.

"Now we wait. But there's something else," he said, reaching into his bag and removing a thumb drive. "Michaela told me the men after you were likely cops. I had a contact in the SFPD download this for you."

He handed it to her and she turned it over once and then looked at him curiously.

"It's the names and photos of every SFPD officer and detective on the payroll as of one week ago," he said. "Go through it and see if you can identify the men after you. It will give you something to do besides sitting around and waiting for something to happen."

"Thank you," she said, and tucked the drive into her pocket.

"You're welcome."

The moment grew silent and awkward before Reese's phone made the sound of an alert. He looked at his phone and read the incoming email.

"That was fast," he muttered.

"What?"

"Your general counsel sent a reply. He's agreed to meet you and promised to not notify the police. He must be eager to see you, too."

Devon shrugged. "He has to tell the board something."

"Maybe he just wants to see that you're all right."

She shook her head. "Keith is a bulldog when it comes to the company. It's why my dad hired him. Trust me, his eagerness has nothing to do with my welfare and everything to do with the shareholders." She paused. "It makes sense that the board voted to name him as acting President and CEO. No doubt it will become a permanent position."

"And you're okay with that?" Reese asked.

She frowned at him. "Of course. It's important to name a CEO as soon as possible so the markets don't get spooked."

"I mean are you okay with him taking over the company?"

She shrugged. "Sure. Keith's knowledgeable. He was Dad's right-hand man. He's been there from the very beginning. Without Dad or Terrence, he'd be the next best choice."

"I can think of someone better."

Devon spared him a quick glance and then looked away with a roll of her eyes, abruptly rose from the desk and crossed to the floor-to-ceiling window of his office that gave a spectacular view of the financial district and the Transamerica building.

"Be serious, Reese."

"I am being serious. Ten years go by and you're still running from it?"

"Running from what?" she asked.

"From what you were meant to do."

She kept her back to him, but he stood from his desk and walked up behind her.

"That company is yours," he continued. "It always was, not Terrence's and not Keith's. When your father retired or passed on, his daughter should be running it. You have the experience and the education, but you never had the courage to stand up and tell him you wanted to run it. Why not? You want to spend your days shopping and going to brunch?"

She whirled around in anger and for just a second, she looked to be startled. He figured she must not have realized how close he was to her.

"That's not all I do! I'm on the board of some very important charities and that alone keeps me plenty busy."

"But is it really what you want to do? I remember those ideas you had to revamp the company and get away from the prescription medications. Now's the time, Devon."

"Stop acting like you still know me," she said, bitterly. "We haven't seen each other in over ten goddamn years. I'm not the same woman and I know what's best for the company. Your job is to just keep me safe, not counsel me. So, stay out of my business!"

She was right that it had been years since he'd seen her, but he still remembered the times she'd lash out at him, and how she always expected him to lash back at her. This was one of those times. She was scared, frustrated and sad, and because of all of that, she wanted a fight, but he wasn't going to give her one. Instead, he gazed into her eyes a moment longer, silently communicating just that and then slowly turned around and went back to his seat at his desk.

CHAPTER TWENTY-TWO

en years ago

"Congratulations to the both of you."

My father beamed at Reese and I, and we sipped from the champagne flutes after he toasted to our engagement.

"Thanks, Dad."

"Thank you, Sir," Reese said, turning to smile at me.

He was smart, sexy, passionate, and ambitious. In many ways, he reminded me of Michaela. He didn't care about my money or who my father was. He was down-to-earth—his own man. I always thought I'd have to marry a man in my own social class who I didn't truly love for the sake of convenience and social, business, and political connections. But Reese was none of those things. I just wanted him, and best of all, my father approved of our relationship.

There was still that niggling fear that this was all just a fantasy and that soon reality would come crashing down, and Reese would be gone. But I was on a mission to ensure that never happened. He wasn't going to be a replay of my mother.

"So tell me all about the wedding plans so far," my father said. "I need to know how much this is going to cost me."

We all laughed, but I wasted no time in revealing all the details my wedding planner and I had come up with. I had hired one of the most legendary social planners in Atlanta, and couldn't wait to tell my father all about it. Poor Michaela had already been there for every meeting to look at invitation choices, reception colors, menu and cake tastings, and best of all, bridesmaids and wedding dress fittings. I figured she deserved a break, and I could torture the men in my life for a moment. However, at times like these, I sorely wished my mother was still in my life. I never knew what became of her, and my father said he didn't know, either. There was nothing more special to a woman than having her mother present during her wedding planning, but I was going to have to accept that it wouldn't happen for me.

When I sensed both my father's and Reese's eyes beginning to glaze over, I changed the subject.

"All right, enough wedding talk. Dad, tell Reese the good news."

He cut into his ribeye steak and rolled his eyes playfully. "I was going to wait until the day of your wedding as a sort of surprise, but I can see you won't let me keep the secret any longer."

"What secret? What surprise?" Reese asked, dividing an amused look between the two of us.

I watched my father put his knife and fork down and dab the corners of his mouth with a white linen napkin.

"Well, Reese, as my future son-in-law, I'd like to formally offer you the position of Vice-President of Foxworth Pharmaceuticals."

"Surprise!" I couldn't keep the smile from my face, but I noticed as I looked over at Reese that he seemed to have stopped chewing his food.

"Are you all right?" my dad asked.

Reese resumed chewing, albeit slowly and then swallowed before speaking. "You want me to be Vice-President of your company? I don't know anything about the pharmaceutical business."

"To be honest, the position doesn't really entail that much responsibility. Like Devon, you have a background in business, so you know enough," my dad said. "Your role is more social. You'll attend meetings, speak with the media, and oversea the managers of different departments. Trust me, it's not as complex as it sounds."

Reese glanced my way quickly and then addressed my father. "I don't have the experience, and frankly, Sir, that industry never interested me. I may have a degree in Business, but Cybersecurity is my specialty."

"Reese," I said, laughing nervously. "This is a great opportunity. The position pays a high six-figure salary. You'd have to work years in Cybersecurity before you'd see that kind of income."

He turned his eyes on me again. "I'm okay with that, because it's what I want to do."

My father leaned back in his seat and frowned. "What are you saying, son?"

Reese seemed to swallow again, and now visibly straightened his back. "I'm saying I appreciate the opportunity more than you know, but it's not what I want for myself. I'm going to have to respectfully decline."

CHAPTER TWENTY-THREE

Reese sliced my ego to shreds when he refused to indulge me in an argument but instead turned his back on me. I didn't know why I was constantly snapping at him, but the only explanation I could think of was that it was still a shock to be so close to him after so many years apart, and I still didn't know how I wanted to react. I was torn between wanting to argue with him and wanting to... Wanting to do things that I, as a married woman, shouldn't be thinking about with another man.

Because Reese knew the city better than either Keith or me, he decided on a location that he believed was safe and secure, as well as some place that stayed fairly busy and where locals and tourists frequented, but also with an easy escape exit.

As soon as we arrived at Golden Gate Park, I put on my wig and baseball cap. I gave Reese a description of Keith, and we both sat in companionable silence, waiting for him to appear.

However, we didn't have to wait long. In just minutes, I spotted him walking along the path looking right then left, apparently searching for me. I started to get out of the car, but Reese took hold of my elbow, stopping me.

"Give it a minute," he said. "I just want to make sure he's not being followed."

I nodded, once again reminding myself that I was out of my element. My mind didn't naturally veer toward the suspicious. I didn't know how to spot a tail, how to hide in plain sight, or even how to stay alive. Everything I'd done up to this point was a repeat of something I'd seen in a movie or on a TV show. Eventually, that little bit of knowledge would run out. How could I ever hope to elude two men who'd been trained to find and eliminate targets?

"All right, let's go. Just stay by my side, and if I get a bad feeling, we end it and get out of here. No arguments. You got it?" he asked, pinning me with a steely gaze.

"Got it," I said, and climbed out of the car.

Keith's head was still on a swivel, searching the park, and he only recognized me when we were just a foot away from him. When he saw it was me under the wig and baseball cap, relief seemed to flood his entire body, but his face turned wary when he noticed Reese.

"It's all right," I said. "He's with me."

Keith nodded. "Let's sit down."

He led me to a bench that looked out at Stow Lake. Reese chose to remain standing, looking around as early afternoon joggers and walkers passed by us.

"First, let me say you have my deepest condolences. I'm so sorry about your father. He was a great man and a long-time friend to me. I'll miss him."

I nodded. "Thank you."

"I checked out of the St. Regis and was about to head back to Atlanta to do damage control." He paused for a moment before continuing. "I wanted you to hear it from me first that the board has voted me in as the acting CEO and Tom Burke as acting COO."

I nodded again. "I read about that. I got access to my company email."

He rushed to continue. "It was only a business move in order to keep the stock from plummeting. You have to understand that with Robert gone, Terrence in witness protection, and you…it's a smart move, Devon."

"I understand. It's what the company needs right now."

I spared a quick glance in Reese's direction and didn't miss him shaking his head in disappointment.

"So, what now?" I asked.

He took my hand and clutched it. "You need to turn yourself in to the authorities. I can't help you if you continue to stay on the run. Also, I didn't want to mention this, but the board is nervous about the Foxworth name right now. Even with me as CEO, the rumors surrounding Robert's trafficking and you involved in a murder and on the run…"

"It doesn't look good," I finished for him. "But so what?"

"What Robert was involved in is all over the news, and I just heard from my assistant that there's already rumors floating that you knew what he was doing."

"You know I didn't!"

"Of course *I* know, but the board can use this information to push for a company name change or even a merger."

My fists clenched against my thighs. "No! I'm not losing the company. There's got to be something we can do in the meantime to stall them."

He sighed. "You can do a video conference with the board and plead for mercy, but frankly, with the DEA and other agencies looking for you, I doubt it will do much good. They are looking out for the stockholders." He continued. "These men who are after you, can you identify them?"

"Yes. That's my last resort. I don't know who to trust in

the SFPD, but if that's my only choice, I'd gladly come forward and identify them. Not only are they after me, but more importantly, I saw one of them commit murder."

"We're not playing that card just yet," Reese said, stepping forward and addressing Keith. "I want her to stay hidden for as long as possible. The board, the stockholders, all of that can wait. You may be the temporary CEO, but you're still the General Counsel and you work for Devon now. File as many injunctions and whatever else you need to delay any vote against mergers and name changes."

Keith seemed momentarily put out having Reese, a man he didn't know, tell him how to do his job. I also didn't miss the squint in his eyes when Reese said his position was *temporary*. But Keith eventually let it go and sighed.

"I'll do everything I can."

I nodded, stood from the park bench and then asked him something that had been plaguing me.

"You knew what my dad was involved in, didn't you?"

He nodded. "I was bound to secrecy by attorney-client privilege. Even if I had wanted to make you aware—to prepare you for all of this—I couldn't."

I nodded, although I didn't like it. It was just another example of my father not entrusting me with the business. Of course I knew he was simply protecting me by not telling me the criminal activities he was involved with, but it only left me with a mess to clean up now that he was gone, as well as a company that I now had to fight to keep in my name.

"We should get going," Reese said.

"Where are you staying?" Keith asked.

Before I could answer, Reese spoke first. "Somewhere safe. You don't need to worry."

Annoyance filled Keith's eyes again. "I only ask in case I need to get in touch with her. I'm heading back to Atlanta this evening."

"I'll contact you," I said. "In the meantime, just do what you can until I can show my face again."

"One last thing," Keith said. "If you really want to know what your father was involved in, you should talk to your husband. I only know part of the details, but Terrence was directly involved."

It was a good idea, but I wasn't sure how many more blows to my father's image I could take. As of now, I was starting to believe I didn't know him at all.

"He's in protective custody," I said. "There's no way I can get to him without exposing myself."

"I understand, but when the day comes that you finally meet with the board, they're going to demand answers. Terrence can give them to you."

Keith then took my hand and grasped it. "Stay safe."

"I will," I said, and turned to follow Reese as we headed back to his car.

"You don't trust him, do you?" I asked.

"I haven't decided if I trust him or not." He paused and turned to look behind him. "But, there's definitely something about him that rubs me the wrong way."

"Dad always said he was a genius and fiercely loyal."

"Yeah, loyal to your father. He may not feel the same way about you. I just have a feeling he's up to something."

"Why do you say that?"

"Because he hasn't stopped looking at you since we walked away—don't turn around."

I snapped my head back to face forward and continued walking.

"Let's just get back to my place," he said. "You've been out in the open long enough."

"He's right, you know," I said. "I can't stay hidden forever. I have a board to address and stockholders to answer to."

By now, we were at the car. He stopped walking and took hold of my arm.

"I get that your father's death put a lot on you overnight, but none of that matters if you're dead."

"I know that, but there's got to be a way I can move around undetected, and I have a feeling you can help me with that."

His eyes trailed me up and down for a moment, and I wished to God I could read his thoughts. He must've realized he was still clutching my arm, because he slowly released it, and I resisted the urge to rub at the sensation his fingers left behind.

"Is this the part where you tell me I owe you?" he asked.

"No."

"Good, because this isn't ten years ago, where you had me under your spell."

I stepped close to him, invading his space. "I never had you under my spell. If I had, we'd be married right now."

He closed in on me, too, and we were now toe to toe. "No, I'd be in prison, because if Robert ever tried to fuck me over like he did Terrence, I would've killed him. It's strange to me that you don't seem surprised or outraged about any of this. Maybe daddy's little girl wasn't completely in the dark."

My eyes widened with indignation. "I had no idea about any of it."

We stood there together in a silent challenge, but I refused to be the first one to look away or stand down. Then Reese leaned in, and all I could do was hold my breath and watch his lips get closer until I could feel his warm breath caressing my face. I closed my eyes, not understanding how this man can go from infuriating me to making me breathless with anticipation.

Suddenly, I felt the car door open and bump against my

hip. My eyes flew open and I saw that he was already walking away to the other side of the car.

"Get in," he said.

* * *

"Daphne, it's Keith. I need you to get me a flight back to Atlanta as soon as possible."

"I'll do it right away. Have you seen Devon?"

"I just met with her."

"How did she take the news of you being named CEO?"

"As I expected, she was good with it," Keith said, quickening his pace. "For as long as I've known Devon, she's only been concerned with her bank balance. Robert, himself always prepared for someone on the board to step in as CEO if and when he retired."

Silence fell on the other end of the line.

"Are you still there?" Keith asked.

"I want to talk about my new role," she said. "I'm not going to be another man's assistant."

Keith rolled his eyes and stifled a groan. "We can talk about that when I get back."

She laughed sardonically. "Those are the last words Robert said to me. He promised me for years—"

"I know what he promised you, and now that I'm in charge, I have the power to promote you, but right now, I need you to stay in your position to help me through this transition. Can you do that?"

Daphne didn't respond for a long time, and he knew in his gut, she was going to be trouble for him. He knew Robert promised her a promotion, but what he couldn't understand was why he'd promised it in the first place. Yes, Daphne was a valuable member of the team, but who was she to Robert that gave her the courage to even ask for a promotion? As far as Keith knew, Daphne had come on board as Robert's assistant with no experience, except for her education. Hundreds of men and women with years of administrative experience and who'd worked for some big names in the Pharmaceutical industry had applied for the position as his assistant. But Robert hadn't conducted a single interview and instead, gave the job to Daphne Coles. Not for the first time, Keith suspected his old friend had secrets and skeletons that had obviously died with him.

"Can you do that?" he asked again.

"I can do that," she said.

"Thank you. Now, send me those flight details, and as soon as I get back to Atlanta, I need to have a meeting with Tom and the others."

"Same spot?"

"The same one Robert always used," he confirmed. "See you soon."

CHAPTER TWENTY-FOUR

Ten years ago
"How could you?"

After Reese declined the vice-president position, the dinner with my father continued, but there was an awkward and tense mood that hovered around the table. I could tell my father was insulted, and who could blame him? Hell, even *I* was insulted. If someone had offered me a position like that right out of college, I would have jumped at the chance. But this man, the first man I could see myself having a future with, had so casually turned it down.

"I told you," he said, keeping his eyes fixed on the road as he drove me home. "It's not the career I want for myself, and you know that. Why would you want me to take on a job I have no interest in?"

"Because it's a wonderful opportunity!"

"For who?"

"What do you mean?"

Reese shrugged. "The way he described the job, I would have no real responsibility. I'd just be a figurehead."

"A very well-paid figurehead," I countered.

"Money isn't everything to me, Devon. You should know that by now. I don't need your father to give me a handout. I can get my own career going, and I guarantee I'll be happier in what I choose for myself."

I wanted to scream. I'd counted on Reese taking the VP position, because I knew that if he worked for my father, I'd have more access to him. I'd be able to see him when I wanted. We could have lunches and dinners together when I decided, and we could take trips at the drop of a hat, because I was the boss's daughter. But Reese working for himself or for someone else gave him a kind of freedom that scared me. I couldn't control what I didn't have at my fingertips.

"You know there are more qualified people he's overlooking," Reese said.

"Like who?"

He took a moment to turn his eyes away from the road to look at me. "Like you."

"Me? No."

"Why not?"

"Because. I—I..."

"You know the business inside and out, and as his daughter, what better way to get you used to running things than to be his right hand?"

"Reese—"

"And what about all those ideas you told me about? You want to transition the company away from prescription drugs to holistic treatments and alternative medicine. Have you talked to your dad about that?"

I sighed. "Once, but I got the feeling he was blowing me off."

I turned to look out the window, and for a moment was lost in my own thoughts of the defeat I felt when I spoke to my dad about my ideas for the company. I still remembered how he simply nodded like an indulgent parent who was listening to their child's dreams of what they wanted to be when they grew up. He didn't take me seriously. I shoved that memory away, once again remembering that this was about Reese, not me.

"Reese, I hate to make demands, but—"

"Then don't," he interrupted, and his eyes were now fierce. "Don't say it."

We sat in silence the rest of the ride out to Milton. It was sad, because I'd fantasized that this dinner would have ended with us going back to his place for our typical hot-and-heavy make-out session like two teenagers, but when he pulled into the circular driveway of my father's mansion, I grabbed my purse, put my hand to the door handle, and paused to turn back to look at him.

"I love you," I said.

He looked back at me, his fierce gaze now growing tender. "I love you, too."

"But being married to me comes with certain requirements."

He frowned. "Such as?"

"Such as you're taking that VP job."

"Devon—"

"That's the end of it," I said, hating the tenor of my voice. I never in my life wanted to speak to him like this, but why couldn't he just make things easier on the both of us and just fall in line?

"I expect you to call my father in the morning and accept the position, so that we can continue with our wedding plans. You're going to love the life I can give you, Reese. So don't let this one hiccup stop you from getting it."

Without waiting for his response, I climbed out of his car

and let myself in the front door of the mansion, confident that my fiancé would adhere to my wishes. In fact, I was desperately counting on it, because the fear that he wouldn't was too much for me to face.

CHAPTER TWENTY-FIVE

The moment Keith landed at Hartsfield-Jackson International airport, he had a driver take him to a restaurant that wasn't frequented by many business people. It was basically a hole-in-the-wall and somewhere off the beaten path, which was the perfect spot to give them some privacy.

By the time he arrived at the restaurant, what started as a slight drizzle turned into the sky opening up and a downpour of rain covering the Atlanta metro area.

Keith walked into the restaurant, which was pretty quiet even for a weeknight. Obviously, the rain had deterred many patrons from venturing outside, which also would work in his favor. He shook the rainwater from his jacket and made his way to a private room in the back reserved for larger parties. Tom, Shirley and three other board members were already inside waiting for him and nursing drinks.

"Sorry I'm late," he said, grabbing an empty seat next to Wendy, an older brunette and wife of a retired politician.

"My plane landed an hour ago, but traffic was a bitch."

"It's all right," Tom said. "You haven't missed much. We

were spit balling ideas on how we are going to resume operations without Robert."

"We may have to hold off on that for the moment," Keith said.

"What are you talking about? We need to—"

Tom broke off when a server appeared to take Keith's drink order.

"Scotch and soda, please," he said.

"What do you mean hold off?" Tom asked when she'd gone. "I'm not giving up a lucrative side hustle like that. Robert showed us all how to conduct the operation. Once the DEA has all the evidence they need, they'll move on. They don't have any of our names, so as far as they're concerned, their case died with Robert."

"That's true," Shirley said. "And it's why we pushed so hard for you to be CEO, Keith and for Tom to be COO. With the two of you in positions of power, the rest of the board won't look too closely into what we're doing."

Keith waited for his drink to be delivered. He thanked the young server and watched her leave the room. Only then did he drop the bombshell.

"I met with Devon earlier this afternoon."

"Isn't she still in hiding?" Tom asked.

"Yes, but she came out of hiding long enough to meet with me. She seemed all right with the idea of me taking over as President and CEO, but she's as headstrong as her father and something tells me she's not going to just go away."

The room grew quiet and Keith looked around the table to meet each man and woman's shocked stares and slacked jaws.

"What are you saying?" Wendy asked. "You think Devon wants to fill her father's seat?"

Keith sipped his drink and nodded solemnly. "She didn't come right out and say it, but I'm wondering if maybe she knows something she's not telling me—something that could take us all down."

"If you're talking about our involvement in the operation, you can rest easy," Tom said. "She's clueless. All she knows is what the news has been saying, and they're only mentioning her father's and husband's names. Besides, even if she did know, what could she do? She's not fit to run this company."

"I wouldn't go as far as to say that," Shirley said. "She has a stellar education, she worked at the offices for her summer internships, and she's attended enough meetings to know the ins and outs."

Tom gaped at her, and Shirley spoke again before he could attack her with his words.

"I'm not saying I would be in favor of it. With her as CEO we'll have a hard time controlling the board and continuing operations."

Tom turned to Keith. "Do what you can to keep her in line. Dangle the profits she'll make in her face. I'm sure money will be enough to persuade her to let us run things."

"I'll do my best," Keith said.

"And if she does have anything against us, find out what it is and keep her quiet," Tom continued. "The good news is, she's wanted for questioning in a murder, and if she's right about these mysterious men after her, she needs to stay in hiding for as long as she can. She can't lead anything, and the rest of the board will agree with us."

"We just need to convince everyone that you, Keith are the right man to take the position permanently. Then we'll be free to pick up where Robert left off."

CHAPTER TWENTY-SIX

Teresa used her spare key to unlock Reese's front door, but when she entered the apartment and saw two sets of furious eyes swing her way, she paused on the threshold, not too sure she wanted to risk entering.

Reese was the first to break eye contact. He snatched his and Devon's empty dinner plates into his hands, carried them to the sink, and proceeded to scrub each one with quick and jerking movements. Devon took her eyes off Teresa and cut them at Reese's back, shooting silent missiles at him.

"What's wrong?" Teresa asked, risking lighting the match to whatever set them off in the first place.

When neither one of them spoke, she turned to Devon, because it seemed like she had a lot she wanted to say.

"We met with my company's general counsel, Keith Hayward, the day before yesterday. He said if I want to know what my father was up to, then I need to talk to my husband. I also need to get back to Atlanta and get ahead of all of this. The vultures on the board are circling and want to use my family's name against me."

Reese cut in, his back to them as he finished washing the dishes. "Meeting with Terrence is out of the question. And as far as the board, you don't need to meet with them in person. There's such a thing as video conferencing."

Teresa turned to Devon. "Wait, back up. You want to meet with Terrence? But isn't he in witness protection?"

"Not officially," Devon said. "Keith emailed Reese today and said they haven't moved him to an undisclosed location yet. He's still here in San Francisco."

Reese put the last dish in the drying rack and turned around, wiping his hands with a dishrag. "It's a dangerous and insane idea."

Devon turned to him in exasperation. "I don't have a lot of options. If I don't meet Terrence, what would you suggest I do?"

"I don't know, but I'm not agreeing to anything that puts you in the crosshairs of these hitmen who are after you."

"You think they'll know she's coming?" Teresa asked.

"They've managed to track her every move each time she ventures outside," he said. "I don't want to take the risk."

"It's not your risk to take," Devon said.

"Have you forgotten that you're a witness to murder?" Reese asked. "You can ID two men who are supposed cops in the murder of a CBI agent. You were supposed to be killed that night in your mansion, but you weren't. Forget whoever it is they're taking orders from, these men want you dead to protect themselves!"

Devon's words turned slow and deliberate, and Teresa sensed she was reaching her boiling point. "I know that, Reese. But I also need answers, and I'm not getting them locked up here in your fortress."

"This fortress has kept you alive. I promised Michaela I'd keep you safe."

"So now, suddenly, you're keeping promises?"

Teresa frowned, unsure of what that meant, but it was enough to silence Reese for the moment. His chiseled jaw hardened, and when he spoke again, he was all but seething.

"This conversation is over. I'm not taking you to see him, and that's final."

"Okay, hang on," Teresa said, stepping between them.

She turned to Reese first. "Listen, it may be dangerous, but she's right about needing answers. I might be able to help. I have a contact in the U.S. Marshals who owes me a huge favor. I'm sure I can get him to set up a meeting."

"Are you serious?" Reese asked. "Putting aside for the moment the danger to her life, she's also wanted for questioning by the very same people who are holding Terrence, not to mention the CBI. Just how big a favor does this person owe you in exchange for not telling anyone they saw her?"

Teresa noticed Devon's eyes dart from Reese to her, and it was likely she had been wondering the same thing.

Teresa leveled her gaze at Reese. "Big enough."

"Do you really think he can help?" Devon asked.

Teresa divided a look between her and Reese, and finally nodded at Devon. "Reese is right that it will be risky, but I'll see what I can do."

"Thank you," Devon said. She then sent a scowl Reese's way before storming off to her room and firmly shutting the door.

"This is a bad idea," Reese gritted. "There's too much that can go wrong. She may not be used to being told no, but in this situation, it's what's best for her, and then here you come, giving her what she wants."

"I'm just trying to help."

"You're trying to help yourself," he accused. "You'll set this meeting up and make sure you're right there to get your exclusive."

Teresa smirked. "There's nothing for free in this world, Reese. You should know that by now."

He rounded the counter and was upon her in a flash. "Yeah, I do know that, but if anything happens to her out there, you can be damn sure I'll see you pay for it."

"Don't get high and mighty on me, you hypocrite!" she snapped. "Let's not forget that the only reason she's even here is because you need her alive and well to get evidence to bring her company down."

The door to Devon's room opened and Reese backed away from Teresa, but not soon enough. From the look on her face, Devon had obviously seen the two of them standing very close together. Something strange passed in her eyes as she looked at Reese. It was such a flood of emotions that Teresa couldn't narrow it down to one in particular. Anger, jealousy, pain, even longing were all evident in her features.

Devon tore her eyes away from them, grabbed her purse from the sofa, and went back into her room. Emma, who had apparently taken a liking to her, followed close behind. Devon held the door open long enough for her to come inside and then closed it again.

Teresa turned back to Reese and watched as he stared at Devon's closed door with his own mixture of emotions dancing in his eyes.

"What is it with you and her?" she asked.

"We're exes. There's a lot of shit between us."

"No, it's more than that. You can cut the sparks between the two of you with a knife. It's a pressure cooker of sexual tension and hatred."

"We don't hate each other."

"Okay then, a very, very strong dislike. But whatever it is, it's definitely smoldering."

Reese turned abruptly to the refrigerator, grabbed a bottle of water, twisted the cap off and then took a long gulp.

He then held the bottle in his hand, suddenly a captive of his own memories.

"She broke your heart, didn't she?"

He scoffed. "No."

Teresa laughed. "Wow. How did that happen?"

"She didn't break my heart," he insisted.

"Oh, come on, admit it. I see the way you look at her, and the way she looks at you—oh my God! It's like she can't decide whether to punch you or kiss you."

She paused to stare at him while her thoughts jumbled around, trying to make sense of what she was witnessing between these two people. Then, all of a sudden, realization dawned.

"Oh," she said, drawing out the word.

Reese frowned. "Oh, what?"

"I did have it wrong. She didn't break your heart. You broke *hers*."

His silence said it all.

"What happened?"

"Can we please drop this subject?"

"Come on, tell me!"

He shook his head. "Why? So, it can go in your next news story?"

She narrowed her eyes. "You know better than that."

He looked at her a long time, and then sighed with defeat.

"She's not my ex-girlfriend. She's my ex-fiancée. Years before I met Beverly, Devon and I were engaged, and the wedding was what you'd expect from a girl with her money —designer wedding dress, hundreds of guests, the big church, the huge event hall with over-the-top decorations, open bar—the whole nine. But when the big day finally came, we didn't get married."

"Why? Did she call it off?" Teresa asked with a slight chuckle. "Did you do something cliché like sleep with one of the bridesmaids, or was it a one-night stand with one of the strippers from your bachelor party?"

He set the water bottle down, braced his hands against the island, and lowered his head. For a long time, he didn't say anything.

"Reese?"

Still nothing.

"Well?" she pressed. "Why was the wedding called off?"

He finally looked up at her and forced the confession from his lips. When she registered his words, her mouth fell open in surprise.

"Oh, Reese," she said, her voice filled with disappointment.

CHAPTER TWENTY-SEVEN

Ten years ago

I sat in the beautician's chair, answering any last-minute questions my wedding planner had for me while my makeup artist made my face out-of-this-world beautiful. My hair was wrapped in rollers to protect the curls, and I was practicing my yoga breaths to keep the nervousness from taking over every inch of my mind and body.

"Your dad just arrived, and it looks like he brought a date," Julia, the wedding planner said, while simultaneously scrolling through her phone. "A younger-looking woman who kind of favors you."

I chuckled. "Oh, she's not a date. That's his assistant, Daphne. She goes everywhere he goes just in case anything with the business comes up. She's about two years older than me."

"Got it. Well, the florist has already laid out the flowers, the pastor is en route, and the cake will be here well before the reception. Plus, some early guests have already begun to arrive. I also see some media vans parked a few blocks away."

I nodded amid all the flurry of exuberant chatter from my bridesmaids, but even with their excitement, my mind was on one thing, or one person, that is.

"And…the groom?" I asked, trying to sound nonchalant. "Are he and his groomsmen in their guest rooms getting ready?"

She looked down at her phone again. "I asked his brother to text me once they arrived, but I haven't heard from him yet. I'll go check for you."

"Thank you," I said, and lifted my eyes for the makeup artist to apply my eyeliner.

As soon as Julia made her exit, Michaela walked up to me with a smile, looking gorgeous in her couture, strapless, Tiffany-blue matron of honor dress with a sweetheart neckline.

"Are you okay?" she asked.

"I'm good."

She studied me for a moment and then addressed the makeup artist. "Can you give us a few minutes?"

"Sure thing. Just call when you're ready for me."

The young woman smiled and moved to the other side of the room to touch up the bridesmaids. Michaela took a seat in front of me and looked at the other women still chatting and gossiping about everything and nothing. She then turned back to me and spoke in an undertone.

"Tell me what's on your mind."

I sighed, knowing she was the only person in this room I could voice my fears to without it turning into fodder for gossip.

"Reese and I haven't been on the best of terms since that night my father offered him a job. He got fitted for his tux, let his brother and friends take him out for his bachelor party, but something seems off. We haven't really seen each other since that evening, and when we do, he makes an excuse to end the night early. He's not the same around me."

"Did he accept the VP job?"

"Yes, but grudgingly."

Michaela hesitated. "Is it really that important to you that he become the vice-president? If he's unhappy—"

"It's very important to me, and you know why."

"I know that you should tell him about your fears. Tell him why you're so insistent that he adhere to this ridiculous life plan you have for him."

"Ridiculous?"

"Come on, Devon. You know what I mean. You have to admit the things you're asking of him are unreasonable. He's not a pet. He's about to be your husband."

"I just want him near me."

"Because of your mom. Yes, I know, honey, but he's not your mom. I could see from the sparks flying between the two of you from that first day at Starbucks that he's completely smitten with you. He doesn't want to go anywhere, and you don't need to hold onto him with the jaws of life. Do yourself a favor and call him. Tell him to not take the VP job and do what makes him happy instead. Trust me, that's all he wants."

I shook my head. "I can't do that. It might be ridiculous, but it's who I am, and if he loves me, he needs to understand that and do what will keep me happy."

She lowered her eyes, giving up, and then stood to kiss my forehead. "I'll go tell the makeup artist you're ready for her."

She started to walk away, but I called after her. "Michaela?"

She turned and I silently pleaded with her through my eyes in order to not give away my panic to the other girls.

She understood immediately and mouthed: *I'll find him.*

But she didn't find him, and it wasn't until two hours after the ceremony was supposed to start that the fears I'd been trying so hard to tamp down slapped me in the face with their truth.

Reese was gone.

CHAPTER TWENTY-EIGHT

Spending nearly an hour scrolling through the pictures of law enforcement personnel with the SFPD had my eyes glazing over. I needed a break. More than that, I needed to get out of this house. It was comfortable enough for a bachelor like Reese, and he had done his best to make things seem less awkward between us. But for the past couple of weeks, I'd been hiding indoors from unknown enemies. I was going stir crazy. I had to stay away from windows, and Reese wouldn't even allow me to take Emma for a walk in the fear that those hitmen had somehow linked him to me and were now staking out the place.

I slammed the laptop lid closed, rose from the bed, and stretched. If I couldn't take a walk outside, I could at least take a walk around the apartment. I opened my door and peeked out to find the large open area still and quiet.

"Reese?" I called, but was met with silence.

Figuring he was still out walking Emma, I padded barefoot from the carpeted bedroom to the cool hardwood floor of the hallway. Our rooms were right beside each other, and I stopped at his bedroom and then hesitated before swinging open the door and peering inside.

I didn't want to invade his privacy, but boredom led to curiosity, and I'd been curious to step inside his room since I got there. Standing by the doorway, I saw that the bed was still disheveled from this morning. I imagined him lying there in a peaceful slumber, the same way I'd seen him that first morning with the covers partially covering his muscled legs and his chest bare and exposed to keep his body cool.

I stepped into the room closer to the bed, and my eyes went to his nightstand, where there was a single lamp, a phone charger, an e-reader, a watch, and a framed photograph. I picked up the photograph, preparing myself to see Teresa's picture or some other woman he was pining after, but instead my breath caught when I saw an adorable little girl with curly, brunette hair. It was the same girl from the picture in his office, only this time she was alone and sitting on the lap of the Easter bunny. Honeybee. She was wearing a white lace dress with a lavender satin sash, ruffled socks, and white patent leather shoes, complete with lavender ribbons in her hair. Her smile beamed for the camera, and I stood there frozen with a ton of questions zooming through my mind.

"You lost?"

I whirled around to see Reese standing in the doorway of the bedroom with Emma right behind him, panting.

"No, I'm bored," I said, stiffening my back and deflecting from the fact that I'd been snooping.

He chuckled, came forward, and gently took the picture out of my hands and put it back on the nightstand. Then his eyes were on me. It seemed to be a habit with him to stand very close and constantly invade my space. I don't know if he was doing it on purpose, but with his body being within inches of mine, my bravado disappeared on the spot. I backed away until the backs of my thighs were touching the bed. That put just a miniscule of distance between us, but it didn't solve the problem that he was still between me and the doorway.

I started to move around him, but since my eyes never left his, I didn't see Emma until I was nearly tripping over her. Reese quickly reached out and grabbed my arm to steady me.

"Thank you," I said. I then looked down at the dog, but she'd turned and walked out of the room. "Is she all right?"

"She's fine," he said. "What do you need?"

"I don't need anything," I said snatching my arm back. "I said I was bored, and because you won't let me go outside to get some exercise like you and Emma, I have to walk around this place."

"And the first stop on your tour was my bedroom?"

I narrowed my eyes in irritation. "I wasn't in here long, and I didn't hear you come in."

He gestured to the picture. "That's probably because you were too focused on my daughter."

"What's her name?"

"Bella."

Bella. Italian for *beautiful*, and she was indeed that. Christ, the man created beautiful children. Now I was feeling jealousy toward the mother.

"Why didn't you and Terrence have children?" he asked.

I shrugged. "We planned to, but I think that was more my dream than his. He was too busy enjoying the money he married into and entertaining his mistresses."

I said it in a joking manner, but Reese's eyes turned sympathetic, and that's not what I wanted.

"Don't feel sorry for me. We were both attracted to each other, and we each had something the other wanted. We got married, and I gave him a way out of financial struggle."

"And what did he give you?"

A way to get you out of my mind.

"Loyalty. He may have fooled around, but he would never leave me."

Our gazes crashed, and I knew without a doubt we were both recalling the same moment in time. But which of us would be brave enough to talk about it?

"You didn't say love," Reese said.

"I guess it wasn't important to me."

"Was it ever?"

"No," I lied.

That was a low blow. I knew it when I said it, but I wanted him to back off, because I was done talking about my mistakes and my failed marriage. But Reese didn't want to back down, and suddenly, this conversation became a contest of which of us could wound the other more.

"Oh, that's right," he said. "Your M.O. is control. You dangle all that money, but there's a catch. A man has to be and do whatever you say. I guess Terrence didn't mind that."

"And your M.O. is running away without a word. Is that why you and Beverly are over?"

"All right, stop."

"I guess it's a good thing Bella is with her."

He snatched my arm again, but with more force this time and pulled me in close to him to the point I couldn't mistake the slow burn of fury in his eyes.

"I said that's enough."

I angrily shrugged myself free of his grasp, stepped around him, and started to walk out. But Reese wasn't done with me. I felt his strong arm circle my waist. He turned me back around and pulled me into him until my body was pressed against his. The fury was gone, and what I saw in his eyes now and felt between his legs made me want to run away.

"You feel that?" he asked, now both of his arms around my waist, trapping me. He was rocked up and ready to go, and I clung my hands to his biceps in order to keep them from sliding down between our bodies and clutching that part of him.

"I want you. I want to fling you onto this bed and drive in and out of you hard and fast. I want whatever is inside of me that feels this lust for you to come out now, and the only way I know how is to fuck your brains out and make you scream. But it won't be enough, so the second time, after we've gotten it out of our systems, I want to go slow. I want to see and feel what your body has become after ten years, and the way you look in your clothes, I have a feeling it won't take me long to cum. I've been fantasizing about you for years. Now you're here in front of me, in my arms, and I can't fucking have you."

"Reese—"

"You belong to him, and I know if I was married to you and any man who talked to you the way I'm talking to you now, any man who thought of you the way I've been thinking of you this past week, these past ten years—I'd kill him."

Without taking his eyes off me, he slowly dropped one hand from my waist, and then the other. He then carefully backed away, as if the slightest brush of our bodies would send him over the edge. Then he was gone from the room, and I was left with guilt, regret, and thoughts of what could've been.

CHAPTER TWENTY-NINE

hree days later

When Teresa's contact in the U.S. Marshals finally came through, I was both relieved and nervous. The last time I'd seen Terrence was at the house in Pacific Heights, demanding he get out of San Francisco and come back to Atlanta with me. It was an ultimatum, and my last-ditch effort to save a marriage that should've ended a long time ago. That was nearly a month ago and so much had happened in that time span.

By the time this night arrived, I'd hoped Reese would have come around and finally understood why I needed to do this. But when Teresa came by that evening to take me to the meeting spot, he walked me to the front door and opened it.

"Ready?" Teresa asked.

I nodded, stepped into the hallway, and then turned to look at Reese one last time. I wasn't sure what I expected him to say—maybe 'Be careful' or 'Good luck'—but he avoided my eyes, simply nodded to Teresa, and then closed the front door in my face.

The drive wasn't too long. In less than twenty minutes, Teresa pulled the car to a stop in an area of town where there was nothing but abandoned warehouses. From our parking space, I could see a black unmarked federal vehicle sitting several yards away with the headlights turned off.

"Let's go," she said, climbing out of the car. "We need to make this quick. My contact is already nervous as hell about this entire meetup."

I didn't say anything, but followed her as we made tentative steps toward the vehicle and three dark figures waiting for us. I wrapped my arms around my waist, hugging Reese's borrowed jacket closer to shield me from the cold. The entire ride over here, I couldn't resist burying my nose into the collar every few minutes, taking comfort in his scent. But each time I did, I thought of that day, just three days ago, when he'd caught me in his room and told me the things he wanted to do to me on his bed. I shut my eyes tight to whisk away the memory, as I'd done at least fifty other times whenever my thoughts reminded me of it. Neither of us had talked about that day since it happened, which had filled me with both relief and regret.

As we got closer, one of the shadowed figures moved under the exterior light of an old and decayed warehouse. The way he moved gave him away as a federal agent.

"Rick," Teresa greeted, reaching her hand out to clasp his.

Rick looked down at her outstretched hand and snorted. "You owe me more than just a handshake. This is a big ask that can get me fired."

"Well, then, consider us even."

"We're more than even. I'd say you owe me two favors now."

Teresa groaned. "Fine, whatever. Let's just get this over with."

He gave her a distrusting look, and then finally nodded to

the two figures standing by. I held my breath as I saw that one of the men was another federal marshal and the other one was definitely my husband.

"Long time no see, Devon," Terrence remarked, looking me up and down with a sly smile. "This must've been pretty important for you to want to see me of all people."

"They can only give you fifteen minutes," Teresa said to me. "I'll be right here, if you need me."

I nodded, and Terrence and I walked a few feet away from them for a bit of privacy. When he finally stopped and turned to face me, I took him in fully and noticed his features hadn't changed much. His rich, dark complexion was still smooth and free of blemishes. He was keeping his beard full yet trimmed, and his dark eyes still held that penetrating gaze that was always hypnotizing and had the power to make me forget that he was a liar and a cheater. I had so much I wanted to say, so much I wanted to ask, but standing here in front of him now, my tongue went numb.

"You look good," he said, "considering the circumstances."

"You, too."

"Are you all right?" he asked. "You had a lot of people worried when you disappeared."

I nodded. "It's a long story, but I'm fine and there's a reason I couldn't make contact. Someday I'll tell you about it."

He glanced briefly behind him at the Marshals and then made one hesitant step closer. He took both of my hands and held them firmly. "I'm sorry I wasn't there for you when your dad—"

"You don't have to apologize. I know what went down at the docks and why. But I'm having conflicting feelings. Should I be mourning his death or grateful, because if he hadn't died, he would've been spending a long time in prison?"

Terrence shrugged. "Maybe. Maybe not. Robert was a smart man. Even with all the evidence against him, I have a feeling he would've found a way to do minimal time."

"And you?" I asked. "I see you made sure you protected yourself."

His eyes turned menacing. "The only reason I turned State's evidence is because he was setting me up to take the fall for all of it. There was no way in hell I was going down without a fight."

"He was really setting you up?"

Terrence shrugged. "It's all right if you don't believe me. He never gave you any reason to doubt him. I, on the other hand, wasn't exactly the most trusting of husbands."

I took my hand from his. "I do believe you, but I need you to tell me what was going on. Both you and Dad kept me in the dark long enough. Now I need to know everything."

He nodded. "I'll tell you as much as I can."

* * *

Vick took a bite out of his steak that wasn't medium rare like he'd asked. But he was more hungry than ornery, so he ate it without a fuss. Besides, his fight was not with the line cook of this restaurant, it was with this job that was taking a lot longer to complete than needed.

Vick didn't get it. She was one woman. Why was it so hard to locate and kill her?

Across the table, his partner, Jones bent over and slurped a spoonful of French onion soup into his mouth. Vick shot daggers at the top of his head. Jones had made a bad call letting Michaela Brown fly out of San Francisco without so much as a scratch on her. If Vick had had his way, he'd have worked that bitch over until she sang her friend's where-abouts. But no, Jones said she might come in handy later, and now they were stuck still playing hide-and-seek with the rich cunt. With every call the client made, he could sense their patience was wearing thin. He made Jones take those calls, because if the client spoke to him out of turn just once, it would be the last time. Fuck the job and fuck the money. He didn't take disrespect easy, which was why he'd had no qualms breaking that Landon bitch's neck. She thought she could fight the two of them, and he was all too pleased to show her just how wrong she was. It had been a rush snapping her neck like a twig, and he couldn't wait to do the same thing to Devon Foxworth. She couldn't hide forever in this city.

Jones's cell phone buzzed in his pocket, and Vick listened with eager interest to the one-sided conversation.

"I owe you, Mike," Jones said, and then disconnected the call and signaled to the server for the check. He then turned to Vick as a slow smile painted his face.

"We got her?" Vick asked, feeling himself brighten up.

"We got her," Jones confirmed.

* * *

By the time Terrence explained the entire intricate setup he and my father had going, I was speechless. Everything I heard on the news had been true: My father had been taking the raw materials from the drugs we manufactured and selling them on the black market for years. Maybe he suspected he was being investigated or just grew tired of the whole charade, but at some point, he decided to put an end to it all and was looking for a way out. That was where he needed my husband.

My father despised Terrence from the moment I brought him home to meet him, and every chance he could get, he told me I was a fool for making Terrence my husband. He was right. Terrence was not the right man for me, but to save myself from the embarrassment of a divorce and being fodder for society gossip, I wouldn't let him go. Terrence was motivated by money. He took to the family wealth like a duck to water, and my father used this when he approached him to be his partner. He allowed Terrence to run the day-to-day illegal operations, but it was all a setup for Terrence to eventually be the scapegoat.

That disappointed me most of all. As a girl, my father had been everything to me—a brave, fearless man who'd fight the monsters hiding under my bed and in my closet. Without a mother, he'd taken on both roles, loving me and being there for me, while at the same time growing his pharmaceutical business. When I grew into a woman, he continued to be the knight in shining armor for me, the man who could conquer anything and do no wrong. Now, I didn't know what to make of him. The flawless image of the man I'd spent years creating was threatening to crumble with every sordid detail I heard.

"I don't know what I can say to make this any less painful for you than it is," Terrence said. "But you should know that despite my feelings for your dad, he did everything in his power to protect you from this."

My laugh was filled with sarcasm. "Yeah, Keith told me something similar, except I'm not so sure Dad did me any favors by keeping me clueless. I've got hitmen wanting to kill me and a board and stockholders who want me to answer for his actions."

Terrence visibly reacted. "Did you say hitmen? Someone's trying to kill you?"

"That's why I disappeared that night. I saw them murder that CBI agent in our house, and now they're coming after me."

"It can't be the Lupino cartel," Terrence said. "They have

enough to deal with now that Robert is dead and their enforcer is in custody."

He paused to think and then gave me an odd look.

"What is it?"

"I've known what your dad was up to for a long time, and took steps to protect myself. But the only proof I had to keep me out of prison was your dad's ledger."

"His what?"

"He kept a record of everything. It was the only way to prove my innocence and his guilt."

"What are you saying?"

"In that ledger, I saw coded names, and I'm guessing they were people that were also involved in his trafficking. I'm saying it wasn't just me your dad was working with. There are others—possibly members on your Board of Directors. Someone wants to continue where Robert left off, and that's a big enough reason to see that you don't take the CEO seat. If you want to find out who's after you, I'd start there."

I thought of Keith and how he eagerly slid into the role of CEO and insisted that I let him continue to run things while I stayed hidden. He was reluctant to tell me much about Dad's trafficking, but he knew all about it. It was possible he could have been profiting from it for years and wasn't too keen on seeing the money train come to an end. How many others were involved, and was Terrence right that Dad had kept the proof somewhere? Maybe that's why these hitmen were after me. Someone out there believed I had the proof and wanted to kill me for it.

I heard a pair of footsteps and turned to see Teresa walking up to us with Rick beside her.

"Sorry to interrupt, but Devon, they need to get back."

"We've been out here long enough. The next shift to watch Mr. Miller will begin in an hour and we need to have him back before they arrive," Rick said, gesturing for Terrence to follow him.

"Hold on a minute," Terrence said, and then turned to me, lowering his voice. "I was glad to hear you wanted to see me, because there's something I need to give you. He reached inside his jacket pocket, pulled out a folded white envelope and handed it to me. I unfolded it and there was one word on the outside of the envelope.

Devon.

"It's from your father's estate lawyer. He didn't know where you were, and since I'm in protective custody, it was easier for him to get this to me through the Marshals."

"My father wrote this?" I asked.

Terrence nodded. "The instructions were to give it to you in the event of his death."

"Let's wrap it up," Rick said, impatiently.

Terrence sent him a dismissive wave and continued. "Look, I don't know when I'm going to see you again, but when I do, we need to talk about what happens with us. Until then, be safe."

I smiled weakly, tucking the envelope into my jacket pocket. "You, too."

He clutched my forearm affectionately and then slowly released it. Together, we began to walk back to the parked vehicles. We both knew the truth. There was no moving on from this, at least not together. Too much had happened, even long before he and my father had partnered in corruption. Too many lies had been causing a divide between us for years.

On the short trek back to the cars, I looked around the quiet and desolate space, surrounded by abandoned warehouse buildings. My eyes trailed one three-story building and glided slowly up to its rooftop. That's where I noticed a shadow sprint across to the other side. It was too fast for me to see if it had been a person or just a stray cat. But Terrence must have seen it, too, and it alarmed him enough to act. His instincts had him pushing me to the side, and I fell to the asphalt, scraping my hands and face just as a series of shots exploded into the night.

I turned my head to the side and watched in horror as Terrence's body jerked from the impact of the bullets and fell to the ground. Suddenly, chaos was all around me as Teresa and the Marshals took cover and began firing back at the shooters, who had an overhead advantage. Bullets rained down, but all I could focus on was Terrence and his dark eyes staring at me and then glazing over as life slowly seeped out of him. I don't know how long I lay there, watching him, waiting for him to show any sign of life, but I wished that the woman who was screaming would stop it. And that's when I realized the woman screaming was me.

I started to belly crawl towards Terrence, hoping to get him to cover, but before I could move, I felt arms around my waist, and I was being lifted and pulled away from him.

"No! No!" I screamed, struggling against whoever had such a strong hold on me.

Gunshots sounded all around me, as I was pulled behind a dumpster, but I couldn't stop screaming until I heard a voice shouting my name.

"Devon! Devon, look at me!"

I was both shocked and relieved to see Reese's fierce eyes blazing into mine. He put his hands to the sides of my face and forced me to focus only on him. "You need to get out of here!"

"Terrence," I stuttered. "Terrence—"

"The police and ambulance are on the way. I'll take care of him, but you need to get out of here. They're after you. Do you hear me? They're here to kill you."

He looked over my shoulder at someone, and I turned to see Teresa kneeling beside us.

"Get her out of here," he ordered.

"They're shooting all around us," she said. "How are we going to get to the car without getting killed?"

"I'll draw their fire," he said. "Run as fast as you can to the car and don't stop."

He then turned back to me, released his hands from my face, and pulled a gun from his back waistband. Without another word, he rose to his feet and darted out from behind the dumpster, firing at the hitmen along with the Marshals.

"Let's go," Teresa said, and grasped my arm to pull me along.

As we ran for her car, I took one last look at Terrence's body lying so still on the ground. I wanted to stay, cover his body and shield him from any more gunfire. I wanted to see if by some miracle, he would move just an inch. I wanted to wait until the ambulance and police arrived and go to the hospital and wait for news of his condition.

Then I looked up from where the shots were coming from, and under the street lamp, I could just make out the face of one of the men. It was the same one I'd seen kill Agent Landon, and no doubt the man beside him was his partner. I wanted to stay and help Reese and the agents shoot these two assholes who'd been after me from day one. But Teresa was steady pulling me to her car, and before I knew it, we were speeding away, escaping the danger that was meant for me.

CHAPTER THIRTY

When Reese unlocked the door to his apartment and walked inside, he realized he must've startled the two women, because they were on their feet and staring at him as though he was their executioner. He didn't say anything, but shrugged off his jacket and tossed it onto an armchair. He then stood in the middle of the living room, planted his hands on his hips and lowered his head to let fly a string of muffled curses.

Soft footsteps approached him, and he jerked his head up to see Devon slowly coming toward him, clutching sheets of paper in her hands.

"Terrence?" she asked hesitantly, her eyes filled with the smallest inkling of hope.

"He's dead," he said simply, and started to stalk past her, but then he whipped back around to face her, unable to hold in his anger.

"Did you get all the answers you needed? Was all of that worth his life?"

She reeled back. "Are you seriously blaming me?"

"You're so worried about that corrupt company and the

money it makes just like your dad!" he shouted. "Is your fucking trust fund so important to you that you don't care who dies while your spoiled ass is kept safe?"

He didn't see the slap, but felt the resulting sting against the left side of his face. He closed his eyes and then slowly opened them just in time to see tears welling in hers. She then slapped the papers she'd been holding against his chest and ran from the room into her bedroom and slammed the door with a force that reverberated throughout the walls.

Teresa came forward. "I don't condone violence, but you had that one coming."

He turned his furious eyes on her.

"Maybe you should give her a break," she said. "Her husband was just shot and killed in front of her."

"She never would've had to see that, and he wouldn't be lying in a morgue somewhere if it hadn't been for you wanting your damn exclusive."

"Fine. Blame me as much as you want, but you have bigger problems," she said, gesturing to the papers Devon slapped against his chest.

Reese looked at the bedroom door Devon had just slammed shut, but he tamped down the creeping regret and lowered his head to look at the sheets of paper.

"What is this?"

Teresa spoke hesitantly. "The day you took Devon to your office, you gave her a file from the SFPD database."

He shrugged. "I remember. So what?"

Teresa gestured to the papers. "She found two matches."

His exhausted body suddenly became alert. "She identified the hitmen?" He now concentrated on the ID photos and two names. When he realized what he was seeing, he felt his blood begin to chill. They were pictures from badge photos, complete with names and identification numbers.

"Detectives Simon Vick and Martin Jones," Teresa

announced. "Devon wants to take this to the DA's office and tell them she witnessed these men murder the CBI agent, Maya Landon, and her husband, as well as the fact that they have attempted to kill her on multiple occasions."

Reese slowly looked up at Teresa, whose shocked stare matched his own.

"She's sure it's them?"

"She sounded sure."

He didn't have to ask. He knew she was certain about what she saw. He just wished to God it wasn't true.

"All right," he said, needing to stall for time. "Let's regroup tonight, and we'll talk everything out in the morning. By the time I left, there were DEA and U.S. Marshals all over the place. Your contact, Rick wants a word with you, by the way."

"Yeah, I'm sure he does," Teresa said, grabbing her jacket.

"Where are you going?" he asked.

"Home. I need to call my editor before the story breaks."

"You don't need to be out there right now. It's too dangerous."

"I'll be fine," she said, putting on her jacket and grabbing her purse and keys. "Walk me outside."

Reese followed her out into the hallway and closed the door just as Teresa turned to him with eyes blazing.

"What the hell, Reese?" she whispered.

"I know."

"What are you going to do?"

"Get some answers!" he said. "What do you think?"

"Are you going to tell her?"

"I don't know. I need to find out just how deep this all goes."

"The sooner you tell her, the better. The last thing you need is her finding out that you—"

"If you were really worried about her, you would've kept your ass here instead of getting yourself in a gunfight."

"Fine! Thank you for showing up and saving the day," she said, sarcastically. "But if I hadn't gone, we never would've known that you're working with the men who want her dead!"

They both went quiet, while Reese was forced to face the truth in her words.

Teresa let out a long sigh. "I'm sorry I didn't listen to you. It was a complete fuckup, and a man is dead because of it. You can say I told you so as much as you want when this is all over, but for now, how about you keep that to yourself and show her some compassion?"

"This coming from the woman who wanted to force her into talking," he countered.

"I've had a change of heart. After seeing them shoot her husband in front of her eyes…" She paused, shook her head in sadness, and then looked up at him. "Be careful."

"You, too," he said.

She turned, jogged down the stairs, and pushed her way out the front door.

CHAPTER THIRTY-ONE

After Devon had gone to bed without speaking to him, Reese snuck out of the apartment and drove twenty minutes to the pre-arranged meeting spot. He parked his car and walked with his head low and his hands tucked into the pockets of his jacket to the waiting Crown Victoria sitting idle several yards away from him. He didn't like the idea of leaving Devon alone after everything that happened tonight, but the suspicion he'd been harboring for days had just been confirmed. Besides, she wasn't in danger right now, because he was about to meet with her would-be killers.

He paused at the rear passenger door, looking around the deserted street, and then opened it and climbed inside.

Silence reigned within the dark interior of the car. Only the sounds of the steady breathing of the three men were heard as they all no doubt reviewed the night's events in their heads. Finally, Reese spoke up, struggling to keep his voice level while inside he was raging.

"When you two first introduced yourselves to me, you led me to believe you were liaisons between me and your boss."

"Our roles have changed," Vick said.

"To murder," Reese concluded. "First, that CBI agent Landon, and now Terrence Miller."

"Miller was a mistake," Jones said, looking over at his partner with concealed irritation. "It was supposed to be—"

"It was supposed to be Devon," Reese finished, his voice rising. "And that's where I'm confused. Why in the fuck are you trying to kill her? Your client wanted a meeting with her. I was supposed to set that up, and in exchange, your client gives me the evidence I need against Foxworth and the FDA. That was the plan. No one was supposed to be killed—not that CBI agent or Terrence Miller!"

"It wasn't meant to go down that way. Landon, Miller, they were collateral damage," Jones said.

"And what about Devon? You've been trying to kill her for days now. Are you telling me she's just collateral damage, too?"

"No. Devon needs to die."

Jones' cold and matter-of-fact tone tempted Reese to pull out his gun and spray the man's brains all over the dashboard.

"Her death would allow my client to get control of the company. That's all the client wants."

Reese thought about what he was saying, and soon felt the truth wash over him in waves.

"There are no reports from the clinical trials," he said. "It was all a fake."

Vick shook his head with a chuckle. "You're finally getting it. We only needed your help to bring her out into the open."

He had been used in a murder plot—a murder plot to take out a woman he used to love more than anything. He clutched the gun in his hand, and the devil whispered in his ear to end these two men right now. But he tucked the gun into his waistband and grabbed for the door handle instead.

"I'm only going to say this once. Whatever deal we had is done. So if either of you come after her again, I'll do what I'm tempted to do right now and kill the both of you."

With that, he jerked open the door and got out.

"You can't hide her forever," Vick taunted, but Reese ignored him.

He walked swiftly back to his car and turned the ignition. He knew they were going to follow him, so he'd have to lead them on a wild goose chase around the city before losing them and returning to the apartment. His main focus was to keep Devon safe and not let her know that he was working with the people who wanted her executed.

When Reese returned to the apartment, he noticed Devon had moved from her bedroom to the living room and was now sound asleep on the couch. He bypassed her and went for his office, where he powered on his laptop. It was time to lay a trap. He pulled up the internet browser and began searching through rental websites, pretending to look for places in the city to hide. In moments, the alert on his computer flashed red. Someone was accessing his computer. But instead of shutting the laptop down and removing the battery like he did last time, he allowed whoever it was to dig deep into his computer while being sure to keep his location blocked. While the hacker accessed files from his hard drive, trying to pin down his location, Reese pulled a thumb drive from his desk drawer, inserted it into the laptop, and went about the process of implanting malware into the files and tracking the mysterious person's location. In a few moments, he had it.

Atlanta. He wasn't surprised, because something told him that whoever wanted Devon killed was somehow associated with her company. Atlanta was where they were going, and once the client downloaded the files Reese had created, the malware would give him an address.

As soon as the malware was implanted, he shut down his laptop, left his office, and entered the living room to find Devon still sleeping on the couch with Emma at her feet. The blanket was down to her waist, and she'd curled herself into a ball, reacting from the cool air. He reached out a hand and slowly pulled the blanket up until it was covering her shoulders. The movement stirred her awake.

"Reese?" she asked, tiredly.

"Yeah, it's me."

"Where did you go?"

"Just for a short walk." He knelt in front of the couch to be eye level with her. As soon as he was close enough to study her face, he saw her eyes looked swollen and heavy. She had obviously been crying, and he felt like an asshole at how insensitive he'd been to her earlier. But once again, he didn't know how to give Devon comfort. Touching her brought back memories of a time he'd struggled for so long to forget.

"Go back to sleep. We have a lot to do tomorrow. I need to get a fake ID for you, better than the one you have, and make some travel arrangements."

"Why? Where are we going?"

"Atlanta."

She frowned. "But, I thought you said—"

"Yeah, I know what I said. But plans have changed, and it's gotten too dangerous for you to be here. The good news is you'll be able to address your board face-to-face. That's what you wanted, right?"

"What about those cops? We should give their names to the DA's office."

"I want to get you out of the city first, then we can plot our next move."

She nodded, paused and then spoke again. "I should've listened to you. Terrence is gone because of me."

"Don't think about that now. Just get some sleep."

"There's something I need to show you," she said.

She sat up and pulled a piece of paper folded into a square from inside the pillowcase and handed it to him.

"Terrence gave it to me this evening. My dad wrote it to me."

He looked up at her in surprise and then looked down at the letter, unfolded it and began to read:

My dearest Devon,

If you are reading this, then I am gone, and my hope is that I had the chance to clean up the mess I made of the business. If not, I'm very sorry to tell you that you will hear things about me, things that I was involved in that will disappoint you and make you question everything about me. But no matter what you hear, please don't ever question my love for you. As far as the company, it would be an honor for you to take over in my position. You have what it takes, my darling. I knew that from the moment you came to me with your ideas and goals for the business. I know you thought I wasn't listening, but I was, and that day, I changed my Will to stipulate that no one but you will take over Foxworth Pharmaceuticals. You are a strong, brilliant woman and the CEO and President this company needs. I can die in peace knowing you will turn the Foxworth name around and make it stand for something good. Unfortunately, you will face adversity from those who don't want to see you take over, but remember that you are my daughter, a Roman Gladiator—a fighter.

You are my greatest achievement.

Love always,

Dad

Reese folded the letter and handed it back to her. Devon took it, clutched it in her hands and when she looked up at him, tears swam in her eyes.

"You were right. I have always wanted to run the company, but I ran away from it, thinking it was easier to just be the trust fund baby. But I'm scared that if I do take over, I'll be just like him. Terrence was killed because I was trying to protect the company. I'm my father's daughter. Corruption and destruction are in my blood."

Reese ran a thumb along her cheeks, softly wiping away one tear that had fallen. "You're nothing like him and what happened tonight wasn't your fault. You're a good person, Devon. You're kind, compassionate, beautiful and beyond intelligent. This is what you're meant to do. Don't let anyone tell you different—not even me."

He leaned forward and softly kissed her forehead. When he pulled back they stared at each other, and he once again, found himself lost in her gaze. But before he acted on the urge to bring her into his arms, he tore his eyes away from her and cleared his throat.

"Go to sleep," he said, softly.

When he dared to look at her again, he was grateful to see she'd closed her eyes. He rose from his kneeling position beside her and looked over at Emma.

"You want to come with me or stay out here with her?" he asked in a whisper.

Emma lifted her head to stare at him, and then lowered it back down and slowly closed her eyes.

"Yeah, I don't blame you," Reese said, and stared at Devon clutching the blankets to her as if for protection.

He went into his bedroom, grabbed a pillow and comforter, and came back out to the living room where he tugged off his shoes, sank into an armchair and rested his feet on the ottoman. As his eyes drifted closed, he watched her, cursing himself for bringing danger to her doorstep.

* * *

"We lost him," Jones said to the caller. "And he knows he's being used to find her."

"At least we know he has Devon, and it's only a matter of time before one or both of them surfaces again," the caller said, then paused. "I never gave orders to kill Terrence Miller."

"I know. It was a mistake. He got in the line of fire."

"Whose mistake?"

Jones sighed, looking toward the car where his partner sat in the passenger seat. Once again, he'd been tasked with relaying bad news, because Vick was too much of a chicken-shit to admit his own fuckup.

"Vick."

The caller gritted. "First he kills a CBI agent, and now a witness in federal protection. He's a hothead and a loose cannon, and this is bringing too much attention our way."

Jones didn't say anything, because he knew what the caller wanted him to do. And just in case he was dense, it was spelled out for him.

"I only need one of you to take out Devon."

Then the line was disconnected. Jones slowly tucked his phone back into his pocket, stared at the car for a moment, and then made his way back to the driver's side. He opened the door and climbed inside, while at the same time withdrawing the switchblade from his jacket pocket.

"Did we once again get our asses chewed out?" Vick asked.

Jones chuckled. "Nope. Just me."

He leaned over the console with lightning speed and jabbed the knife into the side of Vick's neck. Blood spurted out like a geyser, but Jones pulled the blade out and jammed it into his flesh over and over again in rapid succession. The move stunned Vick at first, but then his defenses and need for survival kicked in.

"Fucker," Vick cursed, while grabbing for Jones' throat.

But Jones wasn't injured, so his reflexes were sharper and on point. He dodged his partner's grasp and pulled him into a chokehold. At the same time, Jones pulled the blade out of Vick's neck and plunged it into a new spot that was now exposed.

Vick made gurgling sounds as he tried desperately to stop the blood from spilling out of his neck, but with every second that passed, his body grew weaker from the blood loss. Finally, his thrashing ended, and he slumped over, still trapped in Jones' hold. Jones kept his arm around Vick's neck for a long time, listening until he heard nothing but his own heightened breaths. He then pushed Vick over to the passenger side, and his lifeless body hit the window with a thud.

CHAPTER THIRTY-TWO

"Drop me off here," Reese instructed the Uber driver. "Take her to the terminal."

I was gazing outside the window, watching the city whiz by, but snapped my head around to stare at Reese in shock.

"What are you doing?"

"Just get to the terminal, check in, and head to the gate," he said in a hushed voice.

The driver slowed to a stop at the curb just two blocks from the airport, and I felt my anxiety begin to rise.

"But what if my passport isn't authorized? What if they stop me?"

"You'll be fine," he said. "I'll be right behind you. I promise."

I wanted to grab his sleeve and hold him back. This was the first time since the night I saw Agent Landon killed that I was alone, and I wasn't ready to be alone.

"Reese—"

He got out of the car and took his carry-on luggage out of the trunk. He then leaned inside the window and grasped my hand. I clutched his hand back, but tighter, and stared into his brown eyes that were steady and assured.

"You need to trust me," he said. "I'm not going to let anything happen to you."

I could only nod, even though all I wanted to do was crawl into a cave somewhere and hide rather than be out in the open and alone.

He released my hand and tapped the roof of the car. The driver pulled away from the curb and I turned in my seat to look back at Reese. He remained standing at the curb and returned my stare with an unreadable expression.

My neck was on a swivel as I made my way to check-in, convinced someone was stalking my every move. I held my breath once there, scared the airline agent would recognize me, and I was petrified when the TSA agent stared at my ID a moment too long. But forty-five minutes later, to my relief, I was boarding the flight to Atlanta. As I sat in the window seat, I studied the faces of every passenger who came on board after me, but I didn't see Reese. I figured he'd book our seats next to each other, but when a woman sat down beside me, I no longer knew what to think.

During the four-and-a-half-hour flight, my anxiety grew. I still didn't know what Reese had planned, or how we were ever going to get into the building without being recognized.

By the time the plane landed, I got off and waited for Reese. Then I received a text from the burner phone he got me.

Take an Uber to this address. Don't wait for me. I'll find you.

Then he texted an address located downtown. While in the Uber, I kept turning around to make sure no suspicious cars were following me. Another forty-five minutes later, the driver dropped me off in front of a two-story brick town-home in a gentrified part of the city. I walked up the porch steps and entered the passcode to unlock the front door. I opened the door and walked inside slowly and with hesitation and looked around the empty, furnished living area. A slight creak on the wood floor sounded, and I whirled around to find Reese had come from another room and was standing behind me.

Without thinking, I dropped my purse and carry-on and threw myself at him. No words were exchanged between us as I wrapped my arms around his neck and buried myself into him. A second later, I felt his arms around my waist, and the way his hands felt touching me and comforting me nearly broke what little composure I had left.

"I'm sorry I had to leave you like that," he said. "It was just safer this way."

I pulled back to look up at him. "I'm sorry for being so high-strung. I've been alone before. It's just these past weeks—"

"I know," he said. "You have a lot going on. It's all right to be on edge."

I noticed two things at once: His hands were still clasped on my waist, and his touch had gone from feeling comforting to feeling electric. My eyes now roamed over his face and settled on lips that I remembered the feel and taste of so well.

Suddenly, the air felt still. I was losing the battle to temptation, and as I moved in closer to those lips, I prayed to God I wasn't alone in what I was feeling.

But Reese saved me from humiliation when his arms tightened around my waist, and he pulled me into him. Our lips met with a frantic feverishness that stole my breath and was a shock to my system. He tore off the baseball cap and wig I was wearing, and my hair tumbled down loose and free. He then grabbed hold of it, wrapping the strands tightly around his fist, pulling my head back until my neck was exposed to his mouth. He then kissed, licked, and sucked at my skin, driving me wild.

I brought my arms up and around his neck. My fingers ran through the mane of his close-cropped hair, and I forced his mouth back to my lips. In answer, his tongue dove deeper into my mouth, and his hands went below my waist, gripping my ass and pulling me to his middle, where I felt the unmistakable bulge in his jeans.

Oh God.

When he ripped a moan from me, I surprised him and myself by slapping my hands to his chest and pushing him back. We were both breathing heavily and feeling lost at the abrupt ending. Still, I kept my hands planted to his chest, effectively keeping us an arm's length apart. I bent my head low, trying to catch my breath, and let out a short chuckle laced with embarrassment.

"I guess I was more high-strung than I thought."

"Devon—"

He touched my hands, and I instantly slipped them off his chest.

"I can't do this with you, Reese."

"I know," he said. "It's all right."

He backed away, but still kept his eyes on me. I avoided his stare and looked around the small townhome, desperately needing something else to focus on.

"This is nice," I said, steadily breathing in and out and pretending I didn't still feel the sensation of his lips devouring mine.

He shrugged. "I know this place and my apartment aren't exactly the kind of luxury you're used to, but it has good security. I hope it makes you feel safe."

"It's fine," I said, "and it wasn't the apartment that made me feel safe. It was you."

Those words hung in the air between us for just a moment before the doorbell rang, startling me.

"It's all right, I got it," he said, before heading to the front door.

He peeked through the keyhole and then unlocked the door. He opened it slightly, exchanged a few muffled words with someone, and then opened it wider to let our guest inside. When I saw my best friend, I couldn't stop the smile that spread across my face.

"Soror," I said, and opened my arms for an embrace.

"Thank God, you're okay," Michaela said, hugging me tightly. "I heard about Terrence, and when Reese called and said you two were coming to Atlanta, I flipped." She let me go and looked between the two of us. "It's too dangerous. You shouldn't be here."

"We didn't have a choice," Reese said, coming forward. "They were closing in on her in San Francisco. After Terrence—"

He stopped and looked at me with a sorrowful expression.

"It's okay, Reese. You don't have to tiptoe around it. He was my husband, and they shot him."

"They? Who's they?" Michaela asked, then looked at me horrified as the answer dawned on her. "Those same men? The cops?"

I nodded.

"His death has been all over the news, but apparently the U.S. Marshals are keeping the details quiet because no one has mentioned either of you," Michaela said.

"I'm sure they still want to ask her some questions," Reese said.

"Well, like everyone else, they'll have to wait until we find out who's trying to kill me," I said. "Terrence said Dad kept meticulous records about everything and that there were possibly others involved in his corrupt practices. We need to get into the Foxworth building and into my dad's office. Only he and I had access to it with a passkey."

"Well, I can only assume your dad's passkey is with the DEA in evidence, but what about yours?" Michaela asked.

"That's where we'll need your help," Reese said.

She divided a curious frown between us.

"It's in my dad's house," I said. "But I guess you can say it's *my* house now."

CHAPTER THIRTY-THREE

Ten years ago

He'd gone to a bar on the seedier side of town, somewhere he knew Devon, her family, and even his family would never frequent. He'd only ordered one drink, but kept staring at it and his cell phone, which he'd turned off the second he knew he wasn't going to show up.

Fucking coward. It was what he'd called himself over and over again from the moment he'd made a U-turn away from the church until after two in the morning, when he left the bar and returned to his condo with his suit jacket over one hand and his tie askew.

After taking a long shower, he sat on the edge of the bed, finally turned his cell phone back on, and dared to read every text and listen to every voicemail. When he saw the nearly fifty missed calls from Devon, her family, and his friends and family, he realized he'd just reached a new low.

The tone of the messages went from jovial to concerned to disbelief, anger, and then finally acceptance. The first thing he did was text his mom and brothers that he was okay and that he was sorry. Immediately, his phone began to ring, and he saw it was his mom. He groaned but answered it, figuring she just needed to hear his voice.

"I'm fine, Mom."

"Reese, what happened? Why didn't you—"

"I don't want to talk about it now. I'll call you later."

"Reese, wait—"

He hung up and ignored the subsequent calls from her and his brothers. Instead, he listened to a voicemail from Robert Foxworth advising him to be on the first flight out of Georgia, or better yet, the country. He then proceeded to threaten his life and his entire bloodline. Reese listened to every scathing word, telling himself it was the least he deserved. He then deleted the message and all other ones until he finally heard her voice.

"Reese, it's me. I don't know what's going on. I hope you're all right, and if you are, then I don't know what to say. Why can't you talk to me? Why am I here waiting for you?"

A pause ensued, and then she whispered into the receiver, *"Goddamn you."*

He listened to her message many times over. Why? Why had he left her like that?

A knock at his front door sounded, and he thought that maybe his brothers had got tired of him not answering and decided to just come over. He took off his towel and slipped on some sweatpants before heading to the door.

* * *

I went back to my room twice before mustering up the courage to join Reese on the terrace outside. After Michaela left, we'd done our best to avoid each other and pretend the kiss we'd shared never happened.

However, when I slid open the terrace door and he

turned around to watch me, I let out a pent-up breath, grateful to have his eyes on me once again.

"You okay?" he asked.

I shrugged and joined him on the balcony, leaning against the metal railing. "Just feeling anxious."

He nodded. "That's understandable."

I gestured to the view of the Atlanta skyline. "This is a good distraction."

I cleared my throat and met his eyes, now feeling uneasy that he was still staring.

"What?" I asked.

"I owe you an apology. The night Terrence died—what I said to you—the way I said it—it was insensitive. Your husband was just killed, and I was being a jerk."

"Reese—"

"No, it was cruel. He was your companion, your best friend, and someone you loved. I should've shown more respect."

Love. Companionship. Friendship. They were beautiful words for a marriage, but it hadn't been *my* marriage. I had cried for Terrence, but the ugly truth was our marriage could be summed up in one word—convenient.

But Reese didn't need to know that, and it didn't make me mourn for Terrence any less. He was my husband, and now, tragically, he was gone.

"Thank you."

He went back to observing the view and then let out a sigh. "I never thought I'd ever step foot back in this city."

"Why not?"

"Too many memories—memories of Bella."

"Your daughter," I said, recalling the framed photo of the little girl by his bed. "Does she live here with Beverly?"

"No, Bella died two years ago."

I sucked in a breath and reeled back as though a punch

had landed right in the middle of my stomach. "Oh my God! Reese, I'm so sorry. I thought...Jesus Christ! How did it happen?"

"Leukemia," he said. "When I first found out she'd been diagnosed, I kind of went into super-dad mode. While Beverly prayed and attended support groups and loved on Bella, I scoured the internet for remedies, cures, whatever I could find to fight it. I guess I must've made some promise to myself that I would be the one to save her. Of course, it wasn't up to me, but you couldn't tell me that back then, and anyone who tried was told in no uncertain terms to fuck off."

He paused, still keeping his focus on the city lights becoming more illuminated with the setting sun. "I'd found an experimental testing program for her. Beverly was against it, but I didn't care. I was on a mission and didn't want to hear anything else. The drug they prescribed Bella was ready to undergo human trials. It was supposed to be some miracle drug that directly combatted the cancer cells. At first, she responded well to it, and I began to hope."

He chuckled to himself. "Hope. That's a dangerous emotion when you have nothing else left."

Tears burned my eyes, and I wanted so badly to reach for him in comfort, but something told me he wasn't looking for sympathy.

"But it didn't last," he continued. "Her body eventually rejected the drug and her immune system all but shut down. It was only a matter of months after the trials began that she was gone."

This time I did lean forward to touch his shoulder, but he moved away just before my fingers could reach him. When I saw his hands clench into fists, I knew there was more to tell, and that I wasn't going to like it.

"Who—" I paused, swallowed, and tried again. "Who manufactured the drug?"

He slowly turned to look at me, his eyes now ablaze, and I suddenly understood the reason for the file I'd seen on his computer with the company name.

"You're investigating the company," I said. "You're looking for proof of negligence."

"The drug should've never passed FDA approval," he said, harshly. "It wasn't ready for public distribution."

"Reese, she may have reacted poorly to the drug, but what about the other participants? Surely if everyone who did the trials reacted the same way and died, we would have had a massive lawsuit on our hands."

"That might be true, but there were only six of us. It was a local experiment, and the families were paid off for their silence and signed NDAs. I was the only one who refused. Doctors, scientists—even someone at the FDA had to have been bought off to keep this hushed up."

"I didn't know about any of this," I said, mournfully.

"Of course not. You had exotic trips and spa treatments to worry about."

I ignored the biting insult, chalking it up to the pain he was feeling by bringing this all up.

"I'll take that, but you still need proof. What does Beverly have to say about it?"

He heaved another sigh. "That was the last straw when it came to my marriage. Beverly and I had already been drifting apart before Bella got sick. Then with my obsession in finding a cure and then my need for revenge, she'd had enough."

"Does she still live here in Atlanta?"

He nodded. "Yeah. She's married now with an 18-month-old son." He scoffed. "That sounded bitter, but I'm really not. I mean, I was. I even accused her of moving on and disrespecting our daughter's memory. I was a piece of shit to her. She had every right to find happiness after what she'd been through. I wasn't really angry with her. I was jealous because I'm still stuck in this anger and need for revenge. I can't move on."

I didn't know what to say. The man protecting me was also on a mission to see my company destroyed. So many questions clouded my mind, with the main one being: Did he agree to protect me just to get information from me? *I should just ask him, right here, right now, while I have his attention,* I thought to myself, but I was so scared of the answers.

"We should get going," Reese said, looking down at his watch and putting an end to the conversation. "Michaela should be back at her office by now."

CHAPTER THIRTY-FOUR

A smile spread across Jones' face for the first time that day as he sat in his rental car, watching Michaela Brown through his binoculars. From his vantage point, he saw her punch in the gate code to let her onto the private property in Milton. The tall, iron gate slowly swung open, and she drove her car inside. He lowered the binoculars to his lap and sat back in his seat to wait patiently for her. After Reese realized he was being played for a fool, he'd cut all communication with him and his boss, but Jones was certain the man would still try to get Devon to Atlanta and hide her somewhere. Jones had known Michaela would eventually come in handy again, which is why he'd convinced Vick to let her leave San Francisco unharmed. Vick had wanted to go after her and make her tell them where Devon was, but Jones was a lot more patient than his ex-partner. He wasn't sorry he'd had to get rid of him. In this business, it was every man for himself, and Vick had become a liability.

While he waited for Michaela, he looked around the exclusive neighborhood. Because of the size of each property, only two other homes fit on this stretch of road. He'd read somewhere that the Foxworth estate was seven acres surrounded by hedges and lush trees, worth over ten million dollars, and it all now belonged to Devon Foxworth. Pair that with the value of the business and everything else her father no doubt bequeathed to her, saying that she was sitting pretty was an understatement. Not for the first time, he wondered if he was going after the wrong person. Doubt was creeping in, and he was beginning to wonder if killing a wealthy heiress was really the smart move. Maybe he could find a way to blackmail Devon instead and cash in on her wealth. No, he'd come too far and was too invested in this plan to turn back now. He just hoped his client was the golden goose he'd been led to believe.

He looked down at his watch and realized she'd been in there for nearly thirty minutes. He thought about going in after her, but when she came back out, he decided instead to follow her and see where she led. She had gone inside that house for something Devon needed, and eventually, she was going to bring her friend out of hiding. An even bigger smile ghosted Jones' lips as he realized just what he could do to bring that bitch out of hiding much sooner.

* * *

When Michaela returned to her office, she quickly let herself inside, locked the door behind her, and peered through the door blinds to make sure no one was following her. Her assistant, Jada, would have left an hour ago. Michaela had explained her trip out to Milton as a last-minute appointment at a client's home and told Jada to lock up and leave early. James had texted her earlier, agreeing to pick up the boys from school, and told her not to work too hard. She hated to keep this from him, but if she'd told him she was doing an errand for Devon, he wouldn't understand. By the time she'd returned to the office, the sun had nearly set. She texted Reese that she had the access badge and waited for him and Devon to come and get it. They had agreed that meeting here would be much safer. None of them wanted to risk those men finding out where Devon and Reese were staying.

Devon and Reese. Michaela's mind zoomed at the unlikely odds of ever pairing their names together again after Reese had stood her up on their wedding day. As Devon's friend, she should've held a lifelong grudge towards him, but the romantic in her knew that something deeper was going on. She knew in her heart that Reese didn't stand Devon up because he didn't want to marry her. He hadn't been rejecting Devon. He was rejecting her insecurities and her fears. They could have worked on their issues together and given it another chance. But fate, as it turned out, had kept them apart for ten years, and she wondered if they were any happier for it.

While she waited for Reese and Devon to arrive, she holed herself up in her office responding to client emails, but her hands froze in the middle of typing a reply when she heard the faintest sound coming from the front of the building. She looked up, straining her ears.

"Someone there?"

Only silence answered back, but Michaela was certain she'd heard something. She put her phone down and rose from her desk with trepidation, keeping her eyes on the inky blackness of the open doorway. A terrifying feeling made its way down her spine, telling her she was not alone.

Sure enough, a dark and imposing figure filled the doorway, and Michaela shrieked. "Who are you?"

He slowly held up his hands. "I'm just here for a chat."

"How did you get in here?"

"I picked your lock," he said, stepping into the light. "Do you remember me, Michaela?"

She did. She recognized his face as one of the men who chased and shot at her and Devon in that San Francisco hotel.

"I definitely remember *you*," he continued. "And what always struck me was how much of a good friend you are. You do a lot and risk a lot for her, don't you?"

Michaela didn't say anything, but backed away from him as he slowly advanced on her.

"I like you, so I'm going to make this easy on you. You tell me where your friend is, what she's up to, and I'll keep that pretty face of yours intact."

She held her breath, hesitated for exactly three seconds, and then turned on her heels and ran for the back storeroom of her office. Just before she locked herself inside the room, she heard his chilling words.

"Wrong move, sweetheart."

CHAPTER THIRTY-FIVE

*R*eese immediately sensed something was wrong as he slowly pulled the car to the curb and stopped a half a block from Michaela's office space. There were blue and red lights flashing from police cars surrounding the building, but what made his heart speed up was the ambulance.

"Oh my God!" Devon exclaimed, slapping a hand to her mouth. "Michaela!"

Before he could pull to a stop, she unhooked her seat belt and was jumping out of the car.

"Devon!" He tried reaching for her, but she moved so fast he only ended up grabbing air.

"Goddammit," he muttered as he put the car in park and got out to chase after her.

They were far enough from the scene, giving Reese time to catch her before she made herself known to law enforcement.

"Devon, stop!" This time he was successful in grabbing the sleeve of her jacket, but she wrenched herself free of his grasp.

"Something happened," she said, her voice rising. "I need to see if she's okay!"

"I know," he said, taking her by the elbow and steering her back toward the car. He pressed her back to the door and cornered her. "What are you going to do, go up to the cops and demand answers? You're still wanted for questioning, remember?"

"I don't care. It's Michaela." She started to push past him, but he pushed her back against the car.

"Then let me do it. Let me find out what's going on. You need to stay hidden."

"You're a civilian, too, Reese. What makes you think they'll tell you anything?"

"You let me worry about that."

Her eyes darted between him and the flashing lights for several seconds before finally relenting. He walked her back around to the passenger side and opened the door for her to climb inside.

"Just stay here. I'll be right back."

She nodded and he turned to head toward the police activity. When he was a few yards away, he finally let the apprehension he'd been hiding from her flood his features. He too feared that something had happened to Michaela, and he also feared he was somehow responsible.

He then masked his feelings once again and strode with purpose to a couple of policemen standing by the entrance to Michaela's building. They started to balk and tell him to back away from the scene, but when he discreetly pulled his badge and ID from his back pocket, their tone changed.

"I'm Agent Hunter with the FBI. Can you tell me what happened here?"

CHAPTER THIRTY-SIX

I don't know how Reese got the information, but we were on our way to Emory University, where the cops told him they were taking Michaela.

"They said she got beat up pretty badly," he said, speeding us in the direction of the hospital. "It's a good thing James came to bring her dinner, or this could've been a lot worse. They said whoever it was ran off when James came into the building. She was unconscious when he found her."

"Did James see him?" I asked, trying my best to keep the fear of Michaela being in danger from breaking me.

"Yeah, he gave the cops a description of him." Reese turned to look at me. "By the sound of it, it's Detective Jones."

* * *

As soon as Reese pulled into the underground parking garage of the hospital, I donned my usual disguise of dark wig, sunglasses, and baseball cap. I then turned to him and noticed the look on his face.

"I'm not staying in this car again."

I knew that's what he wanted me to do while he went inside, but I couldn't agree to that. I knew he was just looking out for me, but at this point, I didn't care who recognized me. I needed to see about my friend. Someone had hurt her, and from the sound of it, it was those same men who'd been hunting me all around San Francisco. When Reese relayed to me the information he'd received from the police, including the description of the man who attacked her, I knew immediately I'd dragged my best friend into my drama, and if James hadn't come when he did, she'd be...

I couldn't think about it. I just needed to see her, and Reese must have seen the resolve in my face, because he gave in without a fight.

"All right, let's go," he said. "But keep your head down and stay close."

That was easy to do since it was a Friday night and the emergency room was crowded with patients. I was able to stay virtually invisible while Reese spoke to a nurse and found out Michaela was moved to a private room. I wanted to balk when I didn't see a policeman standing guard outside her room, but otherwise I wouldn't have been able to see her.

Reese opened the door to her room, peeked inside, and then held it open for me to go inside. When I saw her lying so still in the bed, I had to stop myself from emitting a cry. Bruises painted her deep brown complexion. Her eyes and lips were swollen, and she had a tube of oxygen flowing to her nostrils. Bandaged cuts sprinkled up and down her arms.

I came forward and gently grasped one of her hands. "Michaela," I called softly. "Michaela, can you hear me?"

The first thing I felt was a squeeze to my hand. I looked down at our entwined fingers and then back up to see that she was slowly opening her eyes to look at me.

"I'm so sorry," I said, unable to hold back my tears any

longer. I broke down into sobs and lay my head down beside her legs.

Amid my sobs, I felt a hand gently touch the back of my head.

"I'm okay, Dev," she said, her voice low and raspy. "It looks worse than it is."

I looked up at her. "This is all my fault."

She wanted to shake her head, but the pain must have stopped her, and she could only manage a soft shake.

"No, don't you dare blame yourself. These people are trying to kill you, and that's not your fault at all."

"But I—"

"Devon, stop," she said, cutting me off, and then lapsed into a coughing fit.

I pulled myself together and hurried to pour her a cup of water from the pitcher beside her bed.

"From the sound of the description James gave, I'm sure it's one of the same men who have been after Devon," Reese said.

"One of them at least," Michaela confirmed, and then took small sips from the cup of water I put to her lips. She moved her head away when she was done and smiled her thanks to me. "He was by himself."

"I'll find him," Reese promised.

"No," she said. "I want both of you to stay away from them. They're dangerous, and I need you to keep Devon safe."

"I'll continue to look after Devon, but they're not getting away with this."

I saw the dark look in Reese's eyes and knew he stood by every word. He loved Michaela as much as I did. Even after things ended between us, the two of them had stayed in touch minimally, but enough to know what was going on in each other's lives. I envied that, because none of Reese's family or friends stayed in touch with me, but then again, after he stood me up at the altar, I cut him and anyone that reminded me of him out of my life.

"I want you protected, too," I said, clutching Michaela's hand once again.

"I'll make sure she is."

The angry voice had us all turning toward the room entrance. James stood there, holding a cup of coffee in one hand and wearing a menacing frown on his face.

"I want to speak to the two of you outside," he said, dividing his stare between Reese and me. "Now."

"James," Michaela began, but he cut her off.

"No, Michaela. Not this time. I didn't say anything when you went off to babysit her in San Francisco and got shot at, but tonight, you were nearly beaten to death. I'm not holding my tongue anymore."

In order to avoid a scene, I quickly turned back to Michaela and leaned forward to kiss her on the cheek. "It's okay," I whispered. "I'll come see you again, soon."

Michaela nodded and I moved aside to let Reese say his goodbyes. Then I stepped past a still-scowling James into the hall. Reese came out after me, followed by James, who closed her room door before turning on me.

"I know you're wanted for questioning, and I've been debating whether or not to call the cops and tell them to come get your ass just to get you away from my wife." He paused to breathe before continuing. "But Michaela filled me in on what's going on. I may not like you, but I won't put your life in danger."

"I appreciate that," I replied stiffly.

"But here are my terms. Starting tonight, you're going to stay the hell away from my wife. I always told her you were trouble. You just use her."

"You're wrong. I love Michaela."

"Yeah, you love her so much, you got her caught up in your bullshit that could've gotten her killed. Haven't you caused enough death?"

"Hey, back off." Reese said, his eyes turning steely. "You know that none of this is her fault."

James turned to him in surprise. "Really? You're coming to her defense, too? I couldn't say this ten years ago, but I'm saying it now. After seeing how her father treated his son-in-law, as far as I'm concerned, you dodged a bullet—literally."

Then James turned back to me with a sneer. "How's Terrence doing, by the way?"

I'd never had a problem with James, aside from his tendency to be a bit too controlling, but I could see he adored Michaela. They'd been married for just over twelve years, had a set of adorable twin boys, and careers they both excelled in. I wanted that for myself, but apparently such a life was just too difficult for me to find or even keep. Still, I never could understand why James never warmed up to me, but I never let it bother me. Until now.

I stepped very close to him, not caring that he dwarfed my 5'3" frame, and gritted my words.

"He was my husband, so have some respect and then go fuck yourself."

He looked me up and down with derision. "I'm going to go check on my wife, who I almost lost, thanks to you. My children almost lost their mother, so do my family a favor and stay away from her!"

He turned and stalked back into Michaela's room, and I stood there seething before Reese took me gently by the arm.

"Come on, let's get out of here. She's safe here, and she's in good hands."

We started walking back down the hall toward the elevator bank and then stopped when I heard my name.

"Devon!"

We both turned to find James striding up to us with something small and plastic tucked in his hands.

"She asked me to give this to you. I hope it was worth it."

He held it out to me, and I saw the access badge for the Foxworth building with my name and picture on it. Michaela had been viciously attacked, but still managed to keep this hidden. I slowly reached for it and clasped it in my hand.

"Thank you."

He looked at me for a while, with only a tinge of sympathy entering his eyes. Then he shook his head and returned to his wife's bedside while Reese ushered me out of the hospital and back into hiding.

CHAPTER THIRTY-SEVEN

It was a quiet ride back to the townhome as I thought about James's harsh words to me. I wanted so badly for Reese to turn the car around, so I could put James in his place. But I couldn't deny he was right in wanting to protect his wife and the mother of his children. She could've died tonight, and it was all because I had sent her to get this stupid badge that I now clutched in between my hands. Then Reese's words came back to me:

"You're so worried about that corrupt company and the money it makes just like your dad!" he shouted. *"Is your fucking trust fund so important to you that you don't care who dies while your spoiled ass is kept safe?"*

Was I really so determined to continue my father's legacy that I couldn't see the danger I was bringing to the people I loved?

"I need you to stay calm."

Reese's words snatched me out of my thoughts, and I turned to look at him.

"What are you talking about?"

"Two cars back, there's someone following us. They've been following us since we left the hospital."

I swung my gaze to the sideview mirror and noticed that as Reese took a right turn, a car several yards back did the same. When Reese took a left turn, sure enough, the other car followed.

I turned back to him in alarm. "Do you think it's the hitmen?"

"I don't know, but whoever it is, I don't want them to know where we're staying. So put your seat belt on. I'm going to try to lose them."

I did so and grasped the door handle just as Reese punched the gas and sent the car flying.

I looked in the mirror again, and the car following us swerved around two other cars and increased its speed until it was inches from Reese's rear bumper.

"Shit!" I said.

"It's all right," he said, his voice calm.

The car tailing us wasn't giving up easily as it mirrored the same maneuvers and stayed just inches behind us. Reese made a sharp turn onto a back street and shot out onto a main street. He swerved in and out of lanes of traffic, ignoring the blaring horns of other cars.

"Watch out!" I screamed, looking ahead to see a car moving into the lane as we barreled toward it.

"I see it," he replied, and swerved, just barely missing the other car.

I looked behind me and saw that the car following us had slowed down for just a moment. It blared its horn as it raced around the driver and increased its speed to catch up to us.

We were speeding down the street doing over eighty miles an hour, and I hoped to God a cop didn't see us. A half a mile ahead, the traffic light turned yellow, and in seconds, it would turn red. But Reese didn't show any signs of slowing down.

"Hold on," he said, his voice still steady.

I stiffened my back against the seat, gripping the console with one hand and the door handle with the other. Just as the light turned red, Reese made a sharp left turn into the intersection just as oncoming traffic followed right behind us. I looked to the rear once more, and was relieved to see the other car still sitting at the red light, blocked by the traffic as we sped away.

Reese checked the rearview mirror, and I checked the side mirror to make sure the driver of the car had not found us. It didn't look as if we were being followed, but he continued to break the speed limit, made a few more random turns, and then finally pulled the car into the driveway of the townhome we were renting. He cut the headlights, pulled into the open garage, cut the engine, and hit the switch to close the door. It wasn't until we were sitting in the dark and quiet garage that he turned to me.

"Are you all right?"

I nodded, still reeling from the fact that I'd been involved in an actual car chase. This couldn't be my life.

When I felt my fear begin to dissolve, I turned my head and gave him a weak smile. "Did they teach you that while you were studying at Georgia?"

He chuckled softly. "I'm glad I still remember all the side streets and back roads of this city."

"It was very impressive."

We shared a look, and now that we were coming down from the adrenaline rush of escaping danger, it was becoming very apparent that we were alone together inside a dark garage and inside a dark car. It was very private, very intimate, and I had to face forward or risk falling into a deep spell from those brown eyes of his.

Reese broke the silence. "I know you're upset about Michaela, but we need to keep moving forward. You'll never be safe until we know who's trying to kill you. I promised her I'd keep you safe, and I'm going to keep that promise. But I need you to stay with me. Devon?"

At the sound of my name, I slowly turned to look at him.

"We're in this together," he said. "Michaela is going to be all right, especially with James there to watch over her."

I nodded again. "Was he right about me? Do I use her?"

"Hell, no," Reese spat. "You'd have to be blind not to see the genuine love you have for her and that she has for you. I've always seen it, and I'm sure James sees it, too. He's just upset and scared that he could've lost her tonight and needs someone to blame. You were an easy target, but none of this is your fault."

"I used to believe that," I said, "but now I'm not so sure. They wouldn't have come after her if it wasn't for me."

"Cut it out. You didn't choose to be in this situation. Your father died, and unfortunately, his crimes didn't die with him. It's all screwed up, but it's up to you to fix it and save the company he built for you."

I shook my head. "I can't forgive him for what he tried to do to Terrence. The father I thought I knew would never let another man take the fall for his crimes. I know he believed Terrence was bad for me, and maybe he was, but it's still no excuse." I paused and looked over at Reese. "I know things got bad between you two after everything that happened with us, but I don't think he'd ever have done that to you."

Reese snorted in disbelief. "Is that why he tried so hard to get me to work for him?"

"That's because he really wanted you to work with him. He respected your skills. He liked you, Reese, and wanted you in business with him. I think he was more upset by the fact that you wouldn't be his son-in-law more than you not being my husband."

Even in the dark, I could see his jaw tighten and his eyes cloud over with anger. "And you were more upset by the fact that I wouldn't be around for you to keep watch over."

In response to that, I unclasped my seat belt and jerked open the passenger door to get out.

Reese grabbed for my arm and held me back.

"Let go of me."

"Wait a minute. That was uncalled for, and I'm sorry."

His words had unlocked a memory, and suddenly, I wanted an answer to a question I hadn't even known I'd been living with.

"Where did you go?" I asked, slamming the passenger door again and facing him. "The day of our wedding. Where the fuck did you go?"

He faced forward in his seat, and I saw exasperation flood his face. He was uncomfortable, but I pressed on.

"Your brothers checked your condo, and all your usual hangout spots. We called and texted you a million times. But it was as if you completely vanished. Where did you go?"

"That morning, my brothers made plans for us all to head to the church together in a limo, but I turned them down, telling them I needed a few quiet moments to myself before the wedding. They understood, thinking I was just getting last-minute jitters." He paused and sighed. "I was on my way to the church, but a block away, I stopped at a red light. When the light turned green, I didn't move. People were honking their horns behind me, and when I pulled forward, I made a U-turn and went in the opposite direction."

More silence filled the car as I pondered his words. It was what I'd been waiting to hear for years, but now I wasn't so sure anymore I wanted to hear the details of how and why he rejected me.

"You've been wanting to ask me for so long, and God knows I owe you an explanation," he said. "So go ahead and ask me."

I didn't flinch from his gaze. He was right. I *did* want to know, but I'd never had the courage to seek him out and demand an answer.

"Why, Reese? Why didn't you show up?"

"Because I felt like you were buying me, and I couldn't understand why a gorgeous and successful woman like you would ever need to buy a husband. You could have any man you wanted. Then it hit me. You weren't buying me. You were buying my compliance. For the rest of our days, you'd hold your money and connections over my head to keep me in line, as if that's all I cared about. We'd gone from a few short months of dating to you planning the rest of my life out for me."

It was the same thing Terrence accused me of doing, and it was a slap in the face to hear two men say those things about me.

"If I was moving too fast, you could've told me."

"No, it's not that. That wasn't the problem. I wanted to marry you. I wanted you to be my wife. I was in love with you."

"But?" I prodded.

"But I wanted to be the one to propose to you. I wanted to buy you that ring, and I wanted to build my own career to support us. You made all those decisions without me, including getting me a job with your father. I didn't feel like I was your husband. I felt like your puppet. An accessory."

It was what Michaela had warned me about the day of my wedding. So many signs I'd been given, but I'd chosen to ignore them all.

"Fine! I have abandonment issues, but we could've talked about it. You don't just leave. I confided in you about my mother and how she left my dad and me when I was a kid. I told you I was always scared of people leaving me, and then you went and did the same thing!"

He nodded. "That's what I regret the most."

"That's the part you regret?" I asked, my voice rising with fury by the second. "You made a fool of me! You made me look like a complete idiot in front of everyone!"

"I know, and I'm—"

I held a hand up to stop him. "Please don't tell me you're sorry, because it will never be good enough."

I sat back in my seat and looked around the dark garage, feeling my anger boiling over inside of me.

"But you know what," I said, looking back at him. "That's not what pisses me off the most. What I really and truly hate is that after all that humiliation, I…I…"

I began to stammer, and Reese finished my sentence. "You came to see me."

CHAPTER THIRTY-EIGHT

Ten years ago

After my dad and Michaela got me away from the church and all the sympathetic stares of my guests, we drove in silence back to my dad's estate in Milton. I couldn't bear to look at the luggage sitting by the door, ready to be taken to the airport for our honeymoon in Tuscany. While Michaela and I sat in the large family room streaming mindless TV, both of us still in our dresses, I could hear my father in his den, shouting into the phone, demanding that someone find Reese.

Hours later, my father had to catch a flight to Las Vegas for business. He wanted to cancel and stay with me, but I told him to go and looked forward to the solitude I'd have around the house. I also sent Michaela home, assuring her that I was okay and that I just wanted to be alone.

"Promise to call me if you need anything, and I'll be right over," she said.

I nodded, thanking her again for everything, and closed the door. I then looked around the huge, empty house, save for a few live-in help who had already gone to bed for the evening. I decided then what I was going to do. I ran up the stairs to change out of the custom wedding dress that had been shipped in from Paris.

* * *

I was just angry, hurt, and desperate enough to show up at his condo. I pounded on his door and braced myself as I heard the locks come undone. In the next second, the door swung open, and I saw my groom-to-be's beautiful eyes, and they infuriated me.

I launched myself at him, balling my hands into fists, and tried to strike him.

"You asshole!" I screamed. "How could you do that to me?"

Reese blocked my blows, shouting indecipherable words at me, but I ignored him, trying to hit him and hurt him as much as he'd hurt me. He must have finally grown tired of defending himself, because he then grabbed both of my wrists and pinned them to my sides. I continued to struggle against him, but he turned me around, pressed my back against his chest, and wrapped his arms around me. Once I was trapped in his embrace, his shouts had turned to whispers, and it was only then that I registered what he was chanting in my ear over and over again.

"I'm sorry. I'm so sorry."

I didn't want to hear that. I didn't want to hear the regret and the sorrow in his voice. It was breaking me, and I was releasing what I'd been trying to hold back in front of my father and Michaela. The tears were flowing fast, and it was all because this man I loved was speaking.

"Stop it!" I cried. "Stop it!"

I pushed myself out of his arms, but he grabbed ahold of me

again, snatched me back into his embrace, and suffocated me with his kiss. God forgive me, I kissed him back with just as much fever, not realizing until that very second that I had been craving this. But soon, his lips on me were too much to bear.

I moved my head back, stopping the kiss, and then shoved him against the wall. I attacked him with both anger and lust, raking my tongue over his neck and down to his bare chest. He tried to kiss me again, but I dodged his lips. Kisses meant love, and this wasn't love anymore. Love wouldn't have left me alone on our wedding day. This was just sex—emotionless, heartless sex.

I felt myself growing wet with wanting him, which only pissed me off, so I yanked his sweatpants down and got my first look at his long and thick cock. For a moment, I was mesmerized, but Reese snagged my attention as he stepped out of his sweatpants and shoved my jeans down and off. For the third time, he took hold of my waist, slammed me into his chest and then raised one of my legs to cradle against his hip. He dug his fingers into my thigh and to my shock and delight, rammed all of that hardness I'd been fantasizing about for months inside of me.

"God, Reese," I cried out, unable to deny how goddamn good he felt.

He tortured me with a few strokes before gripping my ass and lifting me into the air. I wrapped my legs around his waist, as he kicked the front door shut and carried me into his bedroom, where he tossed me onto the bed. The moment he joined me, I quickly rolled on top and straddled him, bracing my hands against his shoulders, and threw all of my hurt, pain, and lust for him into my hips as I rode him hard and ruthless.

"Dev, slow down," he said, gripping my hips and seeking control.

I pressed my palm against his mouth, shutting him up, and leaned down to hiss into his face.

"You were supposed to be mine tonight. I may have lost out on my wedding, but I want my wedding night."

I slowly took my hand from his mouth, and for a moment, we looked at each other, saying so much in our eyes. Then, suddenly, I reeled back and slapped him as hard as I could. It was like hitting stone. His face barely moved, but to my horror, tears stung my eyes from the memories of humiliation that the man I loved had left me, and despair that the man I loved didn't love me. But I held them back, refusing to let anymore salty tears fall for him.

But one slap didn't make me feel any better. I swung my hand to send him another one, but Reese, fast as lightning, snatched my wrist in midair, rose up, and flipped me over so that I was now underneath him. I tried to strike him with my other free hand, but he grabbed that one, too, locked them together and slammed them down onto the bed above my head. We then watched each other with matching intensity as he thrust in and out of me with abandon. It didn't take long before we were both moaning and screaming for each other as we came.

Afterwards, we continued to stare at each other, our breaths co-mingling. Then Reese leaned down, once again trying for to kiss me, but I turned my head away and began to stir, indicating to him that I was ready to get up. No words were exchanged between us as I got dressed, but I could feel his eyes burning into my back as he remained on the bed. It wasn't until I grabbed my purse and headed for the front door that he pulled himself out of bed and raced after me. Both of our hands reached the door handle at the same time, and I snatched mine away, no longer wanting to feel his touch.

"Stay, please," he said. "We need to talk."

"You said more than enough when you didn't show," I said, refusing to look at him. "Move."

I shoved my body weight against his, which would have barely moved him if he hadn't moved out of the way himself. I threw open the door and walked away with as much feigned dignity as I could muster, when in reality, I was dying inside.

CHAPTER THIRTY-NINE

Reese entered the townhouse first. The place had a good security system, and the owner used an app that Reese had downloaded to his phone that could tell him whether the alarm had been tripped while they were out. According to the cameras and the app, the townhouse had gone undisturbed since earlier that evening when they'd left for Midtown. But he wasn't taking any chances.

He had Devon wait by the door while he searched the place from bottom to top and made sure all doors and windows were still locked. When he came downstairs after searching the upstairs bedrooms, he nodded to Devon, who had remained in the same spot where he'd left her.

"All clear."

She nodded once, stepped past him, and went upstairs without a word. He turned and watched her until she disappeared on the second landing. He then heaved a sigh, removed his jacket, and tugged off his sneakers. He went to sit at the small card table in the corner of the family room that served as his makeshift office, opened his laptop and began reading through his work emails.

It took him ten minutes to read the first email, because even though his eyes were seeing the words, his mind wasn't processing any of it. He couldn't concentrate on anything, and it was all because of the woman upstairs.

After that night at his condo ten years ago, he'd never seen or heard from her again. They didn't exactly run in the same social circles, so avoiding her had been relatively simple, but hell on his heart.

Weeks had turned to months and months to years, but not a day went by that he didn't have a passing thought about her. He loved her, and for a long time, he stayed in love with her. Too many times to count, he found himself swiping through pictures on his phone of her or the two of them together. He'd stare at her saved number in his phone and even began to dial it, but after that night they'd fucked on what was ironically supposed to be their wedding night, and the way she walked out, he was sure she'd prefer never to hear from him again. He was absolutely certain she hoped he ate shit and died.

Even if he did try to make amends, he knew she would never be able to trust that he'd be there for her, so it was best he let her go to find someone who wouldn't let her down. So, to stop torturing himself, he finally deleted the pictures, her phone number, and removed himself from her social media followers.

Years later, when he'd heard through the grapevine that she'd gotten married, he did his best to keep the jealousy from eating him alive. He had Beverly, Bella, and a good career. He was happy, but that stabbing pain of regret still lived within him.

Soft fingers suddenly caressed his shoulder, and he turned in the chair to see her standing before him. The lights were switched off on the main floor, but he'd opened the curtains to let the light of the full moon in. On this cloudless night, he could clearly outline the silhouette of her curves in the nightshirt that barely skimmed her upper thighs. She'd removed the wig again and brushed out her black hair, which was now tousled and cascading down to just below her shoulders with its loose waves framing her face. It was an image he would burn into his mind for years of fantasies to come, and God help him, she was standing within his reach.

"I know what a spoiled brat I was back then," she said. "I wanted to keep you near me, but it wasn't just simply for control. I genuinely couldn't stand being without you for too long. You could've asked anything of me, and I would've done it for you in a heartbeat. You say you're no longer under my spell, but the truth is, you had me under *your* spell. You still do."

"Stop," he said. "Stop talking and go to bed."

"Why?"

"Because you can tempt me without even trying. It's been a struggle for me to keep my hands off of you, so the last thing I need is for you to say that to me and look at me that way."

"Reese—"

He slammed a fist onto the table out of frustration. His body was at war with itself. "I can't keep telling myself no when it comes to you."

"Then don't."

He looked up at her with eyes pleading for her to turn around and go upstairs, but she remained steadfast, silently daring him to touch her. Not sure whether to feel defeated or victorious, he reached out and grabbed one of her hands and slowly tugged her toward him. He leaned his head forward until he was resting it against her abdomen. With his head bent low, he brought one of her hands to his mouth and kissed it. With her other hand, he felt her gentle fingers stroke the top of his head, combing their way through his hair. He closed his eyes, reveling in her touch, and it didn't take long before he needed all of her.

He turned her around until her back was facing him and slowly brought her down to his lap. With one hand grasping her waist, he used the other to move her hair from her neck, leaving it exposed to his mouth. He left a trail of kisses there while slowly unbuttoning the nightshirt she wore. He then pulled the shirt apart and lowered it down to her elbows and baring her breasts. While he made love to the inner crook of her neck and bare shoulders, his hands paid homage to her breasts and his fingers tickled her tender nipples.

"Reese," she whispered, placing one of her hands to the back of his head and leaning her body against him.

His hands left her breasts, trailed down her stomach to her waist, and even lower to her hips. With one swift movement, he pulled her brown thighs apart until her legs were spread and draped over each of his knees.

Then he cupped the side of her face and angled it toward him. "Open your eyes and look at me."

Devon slowly opened her eyes, and it made his dick even harder the way she gave all of her attention to him. She looked at him as if he were the only man in the world—the only man in *her* world.

Without breaking eye contact, he moved his free hand to her inner thigh and lightly danced his fingers along that hot and oh-so-wet center of hers.

He watched with fascination as her eyelids fluttered and her pupils rolled to the back of her head. With his middle finger, he found the tiny nub and caressed it with feather-light touches. Devon squirmed in his lap, but Reese ensured her eyes stayed on him.

"This is what happens when you walk around with no panties," he whispered into her mouth before covering her full and tender lips with his own.

The kiss was fire. She attacked him, while at the same time urging him to continue the erotic dance of his fingers. Reese did so, slowly increasing the pressure and speed.

He gripped the back of her neck and kept the kiss going even when he could feel her body getting closer and closer to release. Devon gripped his arms while her body jerked and convulsed. When he plunged two fingers into her, she screamed into his mouth, and he finally let her go to enjoy the sight she made as her orgasm washed over her.

After she floated down from her bliss, Reese stood her up and ushered her up the stairs to his room, where he finished completely undressing them both. He lay down on the bed, pulling her with him and atop him. Just like that last night he'd spent with her, he allowed her to ride him, only this time, he'd stay in control, setting their rhythm and pace to a point that had her crying out for him, and him never wanting to release her.

"Reese!" she moaned, moving up and down his shaft.

He kept his hands firmly planted on her hips, guiding her, rocking her, and trying his best to not shout out just how much he'd missed her and that he'd never stopped wanting her.

From below, his eyes rose from her stomach to her breasts and finally to her face. She was staring down at him, and he wondered if she was remembering that night just as he was. They were in the exact same position, only then he'd seen in her eyes both lust and pain—pain he'd put there. Tonight, however, ten years later, she was regarding him with lust and...damn.

Reese sat up in the bed, grasped her by the back of the neck and kissed her. When he felt her hands going for the sides of his face, he flipped her over until she was on her knees. He wasted no time positioning himself behind her full, round ass. He stroked himself, once, twice, and then entered her.

Devon cried out for him again as he moved in and out of her, delivering powerful strokes. He greedily indulged himself, trying to lose himself within her, trying to run away from that look in her eyes. It was a look from long ago. A look he'd kept locked in a vault of memories he didn't want to relive. A look he recognized and once cherished. Lust and…love.

* * *

Devon lay against Reese's chest with her arms draped lazily over his torso. He ran his fingers through her soft hair, wishing he had a remote that could shut the rest of the world off or freeze it in time so they could remain like this forever. But once again, his thoughts intruded, reminding him that the woman in his arms was in danger. Someone wanted her dead, and he had been doing their bidding.

She raised her head to look up at him, and he was instantly captivated by her dark eyes reflecting the moonlight.

"You okay?" she asked.

"I was a coward to leave you there alone to be humiliated. I should have come to you and told you how I was feeling. No, fuck that, I should have stood up at that altar with you, held your hand, and together we would've told our family and friends that we needed to work some things out before going through with it. I should have been upfront with you. I'm a different man now. I'll tell you when I'm upset, when I'm happy, or when I just need to be alone. You won't have to wonder."

He paused, looking into her eyes, and then lower to her

breasts swelling over the hem of the bed sheet. "And you'll know when I want you."

Without a word, she slowly climbed atop him, and they kissed passionately. As he felt himself grow hard again, Devon pulled away and looked at him with a frown.

"What's wrong?" he asked.

She cocked her head to the side. "Do you hear that?"

He perked his ears up to listen, and then heard it, too. A soft, continuous pinging sound coming from downstairs. A few seconds more, and he knew what it was.

"Shit," he muttered, gently moving her off of him and getting out of bed.

"What's that sound?" she asked.

"Something I installed on my computer," he said, slipping on a pair of jeans. "Give me a minute."

He left the bedroom and padded downstairs to where he'd left his laptop. As he got closer, the constant pinging sound grew louder, alerting him that the malware he'd implanted had been opened.

"I got you, you son of a bitch," he muttered.

The mysterious client he'd been speaking to these past few weeks was finally opening the documents he or she had stolen from Reese's computer. All he needed was for them to keep searching while the malware ran a trace and gave him their real time location.

Just a few more seconds and…done!

Reese smiled to himself as he waited in anticipation for the trace to return with a location. Then his smile slowly faded when he saw just where the trace was coming from.

"You've got to be kidding me," he said, and sat forward to brace his elbows on the desk.

"That's the address to the corporate office."

Reese whirled around in his seat to find Devon standing

behind him, wearing his T-shirt and reading over his shoulder. "What is this?"

He cursed inwardly. He didn't want her to find out this way. He wasn't ready to tell her the whole truth, but he would in his own time and in his own way. For now, he at least owed her part of an explanation.

"I have reason to believe that someone in that building is the person who's been ordering the hitmen around. Someone who works in your company wants you dead."

She stepped back, her eyes wide with shock. "It's just like Terrence said. Who is it?"

"I don't know. All I could get is the address and the suite number." He paused and turned back to the monitor. "I don't suppose you know who suite 1812 belongs to, do you?"

When she didn't answer, Reese turned back to look at her.

"That's my dad's office, but it's supposed to be empty."

"Well, someone is in there right now," he said. "Someone else has a passkey that we don't know about."

"It's after midnight. Who would be there at this time of night?"

Without waiting for an answer, she turned and jogged back up the stairs.

"Where are you going?" he called.

"To get dressed."

Reese rose from his seat and ran up the stairs after her. He paused to lean against the doorframe of the master bedroom and watched as she shrugged off his borrowed shirt. For just a moment, before she dressed in her bra and panties, he was mesmerized by her naked body. During their entire courtship, he'd been limited to couch sessions with her, in which they kept their clothes on but made each other hot with wanting by rubbing against each other and feeling each other up. Each night after leaving her, he'd return home, get in bed, and fantasize about her soft and flawless brown skin while stroking himself to release. Now, finally, years later, he was seeing all of her. He had felt all of her, and he was ready for more.

"How did you trace the signal?" she asked.

"It's part of my job," he said, not taking his eyes away from hers.

"You don't have access to our systems."

"I didn't need access."

She slipped on the jeans and shirt she'd been wearing this evening and finger-combed the tangles from her hair.

"I don't understand."

Reese came away from the doorframe and moved to stand directly in front of her. He cupped one side of her face in his hand and leaned in to taste her lips. He wanted to devour her, but his fantasies would have to wait, because he was still trapped in a reality in which he was not being completely honest with her.

"Let's just find whoever it is that's after you. Then, we can talk."

She nodded, but he could see in her eyes that she was determined to find out his secrets one way or another.

CHAPTER FORTY

"We need to stop at least a block away from the building," Devon said. "Any closer, and the cameras will see us."

Reese nodded and parallel parked along the curb a quarter of a mile east of the building. He switched off the ignition and leaned across her to open the glove compartment. He saw her eyes widen when he grabbed the gun from inside.

"We don't know what we're going to find in there," he said.

"How did you get that on the plane?" she asked.

He deliberately avoided the question, checked the clip, slapped it back in place, and then tucked the gun inside the back waistband of his jeans.

"Let's go."

He grabbed his laptop case, climbed out of the car, and took her by the hand. Together they briskly walked the quarter mile along the silent downtown street.

"The access badge will get us in through the back, but

security will be notified," she said. "They'll know we're inside."

"We'll worry about that later," he said. "Let's just get to Robert's office."

They made a left at the corner and soon approached the rear of the building. Devon quickly scanned her badge at the reader, and a green light came on and unlocked the door. Reese swiftly pulled it open, ushered her inside, and looked around to make sure they weren't being watched or followed before shutting the door behind him. He then followed her through the dark and quiet hall until they came to a bank of private elevators. This time, she scanned the badge and pushed the button to the executive suites. They didn't say a word to each other as the elevator made its ascent. When it stopped on the 18th floor, she started to move closer to the doors, but Reese put an arm out to hold her back while pulling the gun from his waistband.

"Which way is your father's office?"

"To the left," she said. "It's the last suite at the end of the hall."

The doors opened, and he peeked his head out slowly. The hallway looked deserted, and he put a finger to his lips while indicating for her to follow close behind. They hurried down the carpeted hall until they arrived at suite 1812. This time, she scanned the passkey in the back of her badge, and it unlocked the suite's door. Reese moved her to the side and stepped inside first. He panned his gun around the room, checking dark corners for anyone hiding. When he was satis-fied there was no one else in there, he set the bag containing his laptop down on what used to be Robert's desk and motioned for Devon to come inside.

"Whoever was here, we must've just missed them," he said.

"What now?" she asked.

"Look around for any hiding places. There's got to be something here that your father left only for your eyes. Anything we find will give us an idea of who's trying to kill you."

"The DEA has been through this place already. They seized everything, including the computer," she protested.

Reese shook his head. "He wouldn't leave anything incriminating on a computer. There must be something here."

He went for a side door, but found it locked.

"Where does this go?"

"That's his assistant Daphne's office."

He nodded, and they went in opposite directions to begin their search of the expansive space. It was about the size of a one-bedroom penthouse, complete with a sitting area, coffee and drink bar, a shower, and floor-to-ceiling windows with a million-dollar view of the city. Reese paused in his search of the sofa and love seat cushions and looked around as if seeing the place for the first time. But it wasn't his first time in here. Four years ago, he'd been in this very office, and it was all now coming full circle for him.

"Mr. Foxworth has a few free minutes in his schedule. You can go in and see him now."

Reese rose from the chair in the waiting area just outside Robert's office and resisted the urge to stretch his limbs. He'd been sitting and waiting to be seen by his highness for over an hour. He knew it had been on purpose, but Reese was willing to be humbled if it meant there was a chance to save Bella's life.

"By the way, it's good to see you again, Mr. Hunter."

Reese stopped and turned to the woman with the medium-brown complexion and oval-shaped eyes that were framed by the black reading glasses she wore.

She chuckled, sensing his bewilderment. "I'm Daphne, Mr. Foxworth's assistant. We met when Devon brought you to the office on occasion. I used to arrange your dinners with Mr. Foxworth, and I was his unofficial date at your wedding."

"Oh, of course" Reese said, nodding. "I'm sorry. A lot of those memories are a blur for me."

"I understand," she said, smiling, and then opened the large double doors. "Go right in."

As soon as Reese entered, he had to stop and admire the huge office that provided an awesome view of downtown Atlanta. Bookcases lined one wall where a sitting area was furnished with a sofa and a love seat for his guests. On the other side of the office was a full bathroom with a shower. It was larger than most luxury condos in the city.

"The only reason I took this meeting was because I respected your audacity for wanting to show your face to me after all these years," Robert said, his back to Reese as he fixed himself a drink at the minibar.

He then turned around, drink in one hand, and appraised Reese before he moved to sit behind his desk and leaned back in his chair.

Reese started to take a seat in one of the guest chairs, but was stopped by Robert's booming command.

"Don't sit down. You won't be here long. Just tell me why you're here and then get out."

Reese could feel his temper begin a slow boil, but he understood the man's animosity toward him. Still, this wasn't about the past. It was about Bella.

"My daughter, Bella, was diagnosed with leukemia six months ago. My wife and I enrolled her in a clinical trial your company was sponsoring. She was given a drug the company was getting ready to manufacture, which was already approved by the FDA. At first the drug seemed to be working. Her symptoms were diminishing, and she was on her way to remission. Then, all of a sudden, things took a rapid turn. She's getting worse."

For a brief second, Reese thought he detected sympathy in the other man's eyes, and then with the snap of a finger, it was gone.

Robert brought the glass he'd been holding to his lips and sipped. He then put it down on the desk, and when his eyes found Reese again, they were full of dismissal.

"I'm sorry to hear about your daughter, but sometimes these things happen in clinical trials. Not everyone is going to respond favorably to the treatment. I'm sure my doctors and scientists informed you of that. If you're trying to insinuate that my company is somehow at fault here, then this meeting is officially over."

"I just want to know who at the FDA approved the drug, and I want to see other trials that were done with it. There may be something in there that can tell me—"

"Everything you're asking for is privileged information. You enrolled your daughter in this trial, Mr. Hunter. You knew the risks. Again, I'm sorry for her condition—"

"Stop telling me that you're sorry. If you were really sorry, you'd give me what I'm asking for so that I can take it to her oncologist and possibly save her life."

Reese paused, took a deep breath, and then placed his hands on the desk, leaning in close to Robert's face. "I was wrong. Is that what you want to hear? I was wrong, I was a coward and a piece of shit for standing her up like that, and I regret it every day. But I can't change the past. Please don't punish my daughter for my mistakes."

Robert stood from his seat and held himself erect, appearing like a giant.

"I'm not punishing anyone for anything. Your daughter is hurting, and as a father, you feel helpless because you can't help her." He paused, and then spoke menacingly. "Now you know what it feels like."

In the next second, Reese would've lunged for his neck and squeezed the life out of him, but then the double doors flew open and the haze of red evaporated when he turned and set eyes on her.

"Dad, Daphne said you were in a meeting, and I'm so sorry to

disturb, but you really need to let me know if we're going to this dinner, so I can tell Terrence—"

It felt strange hearing her voice and seeing her face for the first time in all these years. When her brown eyes transfixed on him, it was as if the breath left his body. Then she said his name, and he nearly lost all control.

"Reese. What—what are you—"

"Don't pay him any mind, dear. He was just leaving," Robert sneered. "That's what you do best, isn't it, Reese?"

Reese turned back to Robert, but knew there was nothing more to be said. He turned and stalked away then stopped at the door, paused, and turned around unable to resist one last look at Devon. He wanted so much to prove her father wrong, because the truth was that if these were any different circumstances, he'd ask her to lunch and get off his chest everything that had been eating him with guilt for over six years. But this wasn't the time. His mind was consumed with Bella, and now hatred for the man standing behind the desk.

Reese tore his eyes away from the beautiful sight Devon made with her hair down in waves framing her face and wearing a flowy soft pink dress that stopped just below her knees. She looked like springtime.

He pointed his finger at Robert. "I'm coming for you." He then blew past Devon and Robert's assistant Daphne, but not before hearing Robert's parting shot.

"Good luck."

"Reese?"

He turned away from the windows and night lights of the city and looked to Devon, who was now sitting at the large pine desk.

"There's nothing here," she said, sounding discouraged.

He pulled a chair in front of the desk and took a seat beside her. It was possible this was all a waste of time, but something told him they were missing something.

"Look, you may not have been involved with the day-to-day business of the company, but there's a reason your father gave you a passkey to his office. And there's that letter he wrote to you. That's confirmation he wants you to take over, and I believe there's something here to help you do that. Did he ever mention anything in passing? Anything that seemed strange at the time?"

She shook her head, bit her bottom lip, and began to fondle the charm bracelet again. It was the same habit from years ago—something she did when she was nervous or deep in thought.

Reese chuckled.

"What?" she asked.

"I remember you used to have a massive jewelry collection."

"I still do," she said, smiling.

"But, with all the diamonds you have, your favorite piece was always that charm bracelet."

"My parents gave it to me as a gift when I was a girl. I saw it in some accessory shop and loved it. It's the one and only time I remember the three of us together." She paused to look at it. "I had a chain extension added to it, and over the years, my dad would give me small charms of the places we visited."

Reese studied the various charms hanging from the chain and mentally identified the recognizable ones: the great Pyramid of Giza, the Eiffel Tower, the Parthenon, the Leaning Tower of Pisa and a few others. But another caught his attention that he couldn't quite make out.

"What's this one supposed to be?" he asked.

Devon looked down at the charm he pointed to and smiled. "The Roman Colosseum."

He could now see the overall structure, and it did resemble the famous amphitheater with its miniature

Corinthian columns, archways and partially intact outer wall. But at the base of the charm was a plain silver casing. It didn't look to be part of anything, but was molded to the charm like an afterthought.

"The colosseum," he muttered. "Where the Gladiators fought."

"What?" she asked.

"The Gladiators fought in the colosseum. In your dad's letter, he said you were a fighter—a Roman Gladiator."

"So?"

"Give me your wrist."

She frowned, but extended her arm for him to take her wrist gently and pull on the silver casing.

"What are you doing?" she asked in alarm. "You're going to break it."

He didn't say anything, but continued to grip the part of the colosseum and the extended piece in between his fingers.

"Reese!" she whispered.

Finally, it came apart. Reese looked down at his palm to find the silver attachment. He then looked at Devon's wrist and saw that the Roman Colosseum was still intact, but it wasn't just a charm piece anymore. It was a flash drive.

Devon was staring at the bracelet and the secret it held with wonder and surprise.

"You said your father gave you those charm pieces?"

She nodded slowly.

"Take it off. Let's see what's on it."

She quickly unclasped the bracelet and handed it to him. Reese pulled his laptop from the bag and powered it on. When the screen came to life, he quickly typed in his password, inserted the flash drive, and opened it. One single file pulled up that was titled *For Devon*.

"Do you know what this is?" he asked.

She slowly shook her head. "I've never seen it before."

He clicked on the folder, and it opened, revealing several documents inside. All were encrypted.

He ran a program from his laptop, and in minutes, the files were decrypted and readable.

"Jesus Christ," Reese muttered as he read through the document. "This is the key to his entire trafficking operation. He's got names, dates, quantities and payouts in here, including the names of everyone involved. This is the motherlode, and he gave it all to you."

"Why would he give it to me?"

Reese shrugged. "Just like he said. He wanted you to take over, and there would be people who fought you over it. But he gave you everything you needed to burn it all to the ground."

She scanned the names and let out a gasp. "Half of the board is on this list, including Keith."

"That's a pretty big motive for wanting you dead."

"But I didn't want her dead."

They both looked toward the double doors of the office in alarm and saw Keith standing there with a gun aimed at them. Reese subtly removed the flash drive, tucked it in his pocket, and stood. He then started to go for the gun at his back, but Keith fired a shot that struck the wall just mere inches above Reese's head.

Devon screamed in reaction, jumping from her seat.

"Shut up!" Keith ordered. "And you," he said, addressing Reese. "Don't try anything else stupid."

"I thought you said you didn't want her dead."

"I didn't in the beginning," Keith amended, and then turned to Devon. "I was glad to hear you say you were going to let me run things. You could've continued in your role as a shareholder, enjoyed your wealth, and let me handle the day-to-day business."

"That's not good enough for me, anymore," Devon said.

"It was Dad's company, and he trusted me enough to run it. That's what I'm going to do."

Keith snorted. "So, now suddenly you wanted to be in charge. Where did all this ambition come from? I've known you since you were a little girl, and you were always content in letting your father or eventually your husband run things."

"They're both dead now," she said. "It's time for me to step up."

"That's hilarious," he said. "With what experience? You get an MBA and attend a meeting or two, and suddenly, you're ready to run things? How long do you think the company will last under your leadership? Do us all and yourself a favor and let the grownups handle things."

"I don't need to prove anything to you, and I'm more than capable of running this business. If I wasn't, Dad wouldn't have given me what I needed to bring you and the rest of the board down."

Keith's jaw twitched in anger as he held out one hand. "Give me the flash drive."

"Why would I do that?" Reese asked.

"Because if you don't, I'm going to shoot the princess here, and then you, and just take it. Or, you can just hand it over, and we can pretend this never happened. I'll stay in my role as CEO and make sure Devon continues to enjoy luxury trips, no-limit shopping sprees, and whatever else rich girls like her enjoy doing."

"You honestly think you can just keep trafficking materials?" Devon asked. "The DEA is already investigating the company. It's over."

"Yeah, that's unfortunate," Keith said. "Robert and the rest of us had a good thing going there for a while. He even had that CBI Agent Maya Landon on his payroll when he decided to move operations to San Francisco. We were making boatloads of money, but then he suddenly grew a conscience and wanted to stop. I didn't care that he wanted to sell your husband up the river. I never liked him, either. But Robert didn't care that if he ended operations, it would affect all of our pockets. So you're right, my dear. I can't go back to the way things were. But as president and CEO, I control the board. They'll do what I want, and I'll make sure to make up for the profits I lost."

He used one hand to aim the gun at Reese and then outstretched his other hand. "Give it to me."

Reese didn't move.

"No?" Keith said, and then shrugged, turning the gun on Devon. "Then say goodbye to your girlfriend."

But this time, Reese did move, and it was like a flash. He grabbed Devon by the waist and dove with her behind the desk just as Keith's bullet struck the pine. He snatched his gun from his waistband and began exchanging fire back and forth with Keith. Too late, he noticed movement out of the corner of his eye, but before he could react, he saw Devon being lifted up into Jones's grasp. The man then pointed a gun to her head.

"Don't move," Jones ordered.

Keith turned his gun to Jones, and Jones fired one round into Keith's head, which sent his body propelling backward and crashing to the floor in a dead heap.

CHAPTER FORTY-ONE

"I came from the side door," Jones said, backing away with Devon pressed close to him. "Sorry to crash the party, but I've been tracking this one from San Francisco to Atlanta, and I'm ready to end this."

"So am I," Reese said, coolly, keeping his gun aimed at Jones' head. "FBI. Put the gun down."

"FBI?" Devon asked over Jones's maniacal laugh.

"I don't give a fuck who you are," Jones said. "But do you really think you can fire that shot before I get one off in her head?"

"Yeah, I really do."

"Reese—" Devon started to speak.

"It's all right," he said, not taking his eyes or aim off Jones. "Stay calm."

Jones laughed. "That's sweet. You still don't know whose side you're on, do you? Her dad and this company are the reason your daughter is dead. Isn't that why you came to us in the first place?"

Reese only spared a glance at Devon, but he could see the realization and horror painting her face.

"That's right, sweetheart," Jones hissed into her ear. "Your so-called protector was actually working for us. He made a deal to bring you to us in exchange for evidence proving negligence in that drug trial. You've been running around with the enemy—"

The sound of the single gunshot echoed like a roar along the walls. Jones's head snapped back, and his grip instantly released Devon. It was the momentary distraction Reese had been waiting for.

Devon screamed and watched Jones's body fall backwards and land on the carpeted floor with a thud. She then turned back to Reese, who was now holding the gun at his side.

"Are you all right?" he asked, coming over to kick the gun away from Jones's body.

She nodded, and for a moment, they stood there together in silence, but it didn't last long as footsteps were heard running down the hallway. Reese quickly pulled her behind him again and aimed the gun at the door. He then instantly lowered it as he saw a woman he faintly recognized run into the office and skid to a halt.

"Oh my God!" she cried out. "What happened?"

"Daphne?" Devon asked, stepping from behind Reese.

The woman looked up from the dead bodies on the floor. "Devon! Oh my God, where have you been? I heard the shots and hid in one of the offices to call the police. What the hell is going on?"

The distant sound of sirens could already be heard. Reese laid his gun on the desk, reached inside his pocket, and pulled out the flash drive. He then handed it to Devon.

"Reattach this and then put your bracelet back on. I don't want the cops to take it from you."

"What's that?" Daphne asked, observing the exchange.

"It's the evidence Dad gave me to fire most of the board,"

Devon said, snapping the casing back onto the flash drive and then fastening her bracelet to her wrist. "We're starting over."

"So you're really going to be CEO?" Daphne asked.

"Of course, I am," Devon said, walking over to where Keith's body lay. "This is my company now, and I'm going to run it. Fuck what the grownups say." She then looked over to Daphne. "I need you to call an emergency board meeting tomorrow."

Daphne nodded as her cell rang. She answered the call, said a few short words, and told the caller she was coming down to the lobby.

"That was front desk security," she said, ending the call. "I need to bring the police up here."

Daphne left the office, and once again, Reese and Devon were left alone. He could feel her eyes boring into him as he shut down his laptop and tucked it into his bag.

"You're just full of surprises," she said. "An FBI agent?"

"I was an agent in the Cyber Ops division," he explained. "After I started my firm, I went part-time and now just do consultant work for them."

"Really? Do you also do consultant work for hitmen?" she asked in a tone brimming with snide and sarcasm.

"No."

"Jones said you were you working with them. Is that true?"

He shrugged his bag over one shoulder and rounded the desk to come toward her. As he got within a few inches, Devon backed up and his heart sank.

"Devon—"

"That's why you agreed to help me in the first place."

"That was part of the reason."

His confession instantly deflated her, and he couldn't stand to see the hurt in her eyes or hear it in her voice.

"You were going to hand me over to them so they could kill me."

"I didn't know they were the men who were after you. I made a deal with them, yes, but it was only to find you and arrange a meeting in exchange for evidence for Bella. But I was played. They had no evidence against the company, and they wanted you dead."

"Why didn't you tell me?"

"Because I wouldn't be able to stand the look on your face —the way you're looking at me right now—that I'm your enemy."

"Well then, what are you, because you're definitely not my ally. You've been investigating my father and looking for evidence to bring this company down. Now I find out you made a deal with two murderers!"

"I never would've let them hurt you. When I found out who they were, I cut ties with them and had to keep it to myself until I could find out who they were working for."

"Well, it was obviously Keith," she said. "He made it clear that he wanted me out of the way so that he could continue operations."

"I'm not so sure about that. He wanted you out of the way, but he didn't want you killed."

"He pulled a gun on us!"

"Only because we wouldn't give him the flash drive. I don't think he was the one giving Vick and Jones their orders."

"What are you saying?"

"I'm saying I don't think you're out of danger yet."

"Keith is dead, and I have evidence to ask the members of the board for their resignation or have them thrown in prison. I can't get any more bulletproof than that. It's over, Reese, and you can go now."

"What?"

"You can go back to San Francisco. I'm going to call my own lawyer, speak to the police, and make all the statements they need. Then I'm going to get started running this company. I don't need your help anymore."

He went for her again, and as she tried to back away, he grabbed her forearm and pulled her toward him.

"Don't act like you're afraid of me because I know otherwise. You know damn well if I wanted to hurt you, I could've done it ten times over when you were in my arms, coming all over my hands, or when I was deep inside of you. You're right that when I agreed to take you in, it was for selfish reasons. I was looking for justice for Bella, but I also didn't want anything to happen to you."

She shrugged her arm from his grasp. "I'm officially relieving you of your duty. I can hire bodyguards if it will make you feel better. So leave and do whatever it is you need to do to get your revenge."

The fury he was feeling was threatening to incinerate him, but he recognized the wall she'd built up, and there was no tearing it down. She'd completely closed herself off to him.

Soon the sound of radios blaring and law enforcement personnel rushing down the hallway could be heard. He stepped away from Devon and together they waited for the police to enter. Amidst the flurry of activity, he looked to the windows and watched as early dawn approached and had a foreboding feeling that Devon still had an unknown enemy. Keith hadn't once admitted that it was him Reese had been sending emails to all this time. There was someone else out there who wanted her gone.

CHAPTER FORTY-TWO

Once the Atlanta police came to take both my and Reese's statements, I was convinced an APB must've been sent out to every law enforcement outfit in the country that I had finally resurfaced. Daphne contacted my personal lawyer, who quickly arrived to navigate me through all the legal stuff and assured the authorities I would be making an official statement at my earliest convenience.

They wanted to arrest Reese, but once he showed them his FBI badge and gave them a rundown of what happened, he was free to go after giving the officers his contact information. I could feel him looking my way, but I didn't return the stare. As far as I was concerned, the two hitmen who'd been after me were dead since one of the officers informed me that San Francisco police had recovered the body of Detective Vick in a dumpster. They were both gone, and for the first time, I felt free and safe enough to step outside. Even more importantly, I could now show my face and address the board and the shareholders as the acting president and CEO. And in order to do so, I had to rid myself of all distractions—and Reese was my biggest distraction of all.

* * *

Daphne arranged for me to stay in a condo in Midtown to sleep for a few hours. The next morning, I showered and changed into a black Chanel suit and black peep-toe Louboutin heels for the board meeting. At Reese's insistence, there was an armed guard standing at my door and escorting me around town.

A driver picked me and my security detail up at precisely five the next morning and before I knew it, I was assuming my father's role, addressing a roomful of men and women who either wanted to see me succeed or fail.

Tom Burke stood from his seat. "Due to the recent and tragic circumstances of Keith Hayward's death, we are conducting this meeting to name an acting president and CEO before the markets open. However, with all due respect, because this meeting directly affects her, I insist that Mrs. Foxworth-Miller be removed from the room while we conduct this vote. I don't care if her name is on the building, this is standard practice."

"Well, I am here," I said, taking the seat at the head of the table where my father used to sit. "So, by all means, please conduct your vote."

Tom shook his head and began the proceedings. "All board members are present and accounted for. Those not present have sent in their proxy. We hereby cast our vote for president and CEO of Foxworth Pharmaceuticals. All in favor of naming Devon Foxworth-Miller as president and CEO, say 'aye.'"

I looked around the room at the men and women. I received eight ayes.

"All those opposed say, 'nay,'" Burke instructed.

I also received eight votes against me, including Tom

Burke. The board was at a stalemate, including the proxies, and I now needed a deciding vote.

"Aye."

"We all turned to the door to see an older, attractive black woman with a complexion similar to mine wearing a tailored beige suit and pumps.

"Mrs. Foxworth—"

"I'm back to my maiden name, Tom. You know that. It's Kane."

"Well, Ms. Kane, the board has not recognized you."

"So, then recognize me. And once you do that, my vote will still be in favor of Devon taking over as president and CEO."

I stood slowly, my eyes widening at the sight before me. "Mom?"

She looked at me with so much love in her eyes that I couldn't take it and had to look away. I heard voices all around me, but I wasn't processing any of it. My mother was actually here.

"Devon? Devon?"

I turned to see Daphne shaking my arm. "What?"

"Congratulations," she said, smiling. "You're the new president and CEO."

I turned to the board members and saw a mixture of happy and disappointed faces staring back at me.

I struggled to pull myself together, straightened my blazer, and cleared my throat. "To all those who voted for me, I thank you, and I look forward to working with each and every one of you to move this company forward and implement the changes that will help it flourish."

"To all those who voted against me, I expect your letters of resignation on my desk within the hour."

Pandemonium erupted around the room and Tom stood,

his body quaking with indignance as he pointed his bony finger at me.

"Wait a minute, little girl, you can't do that! Most of us have been on this board since your father started this business in his shed. You can't just throw us all out into the streets because we voted against you. We vote for whatever's in the best interest of this company and its shareholders. So stop the tantrum and grow up!"

"That's where you're wrong, Tom," I said, narrowing my gaze at him. "I'm not throwing you out because you voted against me. I'm throwing you all out because you're a bunch of thieves."

"What are you talking about?" Shirley Fallon asked, rising from her seat.

"Daphne, would you mind?"

She nodded at my request, went to the doors of the conference room, and opened them. Immediately, DEA agents swarmed the room, arresting eight men and women. The same men and women my father named in his files as co-conspirators in his drug trafficking operation.

"This board meeting has officially concluded," I said, speaking over the melee.

"If your father were here—" Tom began as he was being whisked away in handcuffs.

"But he's not here," I said. "Now get out of my building. This little girl has a company to run."

One by one, I shook the hands of the remaining men and women and accepted their congratulations, until finally, Daphne, my mom, and I were the only ones left in the room.

Daphne looked between the two of us and then cleared her throat awkwardly. "I need to meet with the PR team and get a statement prepared for you," she said. "You're going to need to speak to the press as soon as possible."

"Thank you, Daphne," I said, and watched as she exited

the room. I then turned to the woman who was my mother and noticed her also watching Daphne leave, but with an odd look.

"What is it?" I asked when we were alone.

She turned back to me. "Nothing. She just looks familiar to me."

"She was Dad's assistant. You've probably seen her at a lot of company functions."

"Well, I was never permitted to attend any company functions," she said. "It was part of the terms of my divorce. In fact, I was never allowed to step foot inside this building."

"But you came to the board meeting."

"Because Robert died, and I knew they'd be voting in a new president. I wanted to support you."

The laugh came so abruptly, I surprised myself.

"You wanted to support me? Wow! After all these years, now you decided to come and support your daughter? Well, I guess better late than never."

"Devon," she said, sadly, "there's a lot you don't know."

"I know that you left us when I was six and never looked back. You never once tried to contact me or see me."

"There was a lot going on between your father and me, but please don't think I never once kept up with you. I know everything about you. I always made sure you were safe and loved."

No, I couldn't deal with this right now.

"Honey, I love you so much."

She came forward and tried to touch me, but I backed away, afraid that a loving and gentle touch from her would break me and make me forget that she hadn't been there when I'd waited years for her to return. When I'd desperately needed no one else but her through all the good and bad times in my childhood and adult life.

"Thank you for voting in my favor, but I need you to leave."

"Devon."

"Please. I don't want to see you."

I turned away from her, and for a long time, I felt her steady gaze at my back, silently begging me to turn around and look at her, but I couldn't. Finally, I heard her retreating footsteps. The conference doors opened, and when they closed, only then did I turn around.

But she was gone.

CHAPTER FORTY-THREE

"I shouldn't have anymore," I said, covering the rim of my glass with my hand.

"Oh stop," Daphne said, slapping my hand away lightly. "I'm driving and your dad used to have a drink after every successful board meeting to celebrate. You're the new CEO, and there's no reason to stop tradition."

She accepted the two shot glasses from the bartender and handed one to me.

"Cheers!" she said, before downing her liquor in one gulp.

I followed suit and smiled as a warm feeling rushed over me. It was Friday evening, and on Monday, I was going to plan my father's and Terrence's funerals and begin my new job as president and CEO. I'd dismissed my security detail and accepted Daphne's offer to go out for drinks simply because if I'd stayed in that condo she'd rented for me, I'd be tempted to call my mom and tell her I missed her, or even worse, call Reese and tell him I needed him.

"You were so awesome in there," Daphne said. "The moment you brought in those DEA agents, you had those people crapping in their pants!"

"They weren't afraid of me," I said. "They were willing to risk it all to not see me in charge."

"Well, thank God for your mom. I'd heard Robert kept her on the board, but she's never attended a vote or a meeting before. Was it weird seeing her after all these years?"

I turned to look at her, and she grew visibly uncomfortable. "Robert told me the story of how she left when you were a girl. It was your first time seeing her after all this time, right?"

"Right." I then flagged down the bartender, needing some stimulation to rid my mind of both my mom and Reese. "I'll have another."

"Yes!" Daphne cheered.

* * *

Reese leaned back against the same desk chair in which only two nights ago, he'd had Devon in his arms and was making her come. One more night. Just one more night he'd give himself to fantasize about her, and then he was packing up and returning to San Francisco. He had jobs with his firm that needed to be completed and some consultant work for the FBI that was overdue. It wasn't like him at all to slack on his work, but when Devon blew into his life again after ten years apart, everything had stopped. She had been all that mattered.

The doorbell rang, and in the deep recesses of his mind, he hoped against hope it was her. But when he looked through the peephole, he frowned. He opened the door and was struck by the sight of an older woman standing on the porch who looked so much like the woman who'd taken his thoughts captive.

"Hi, Reese. I'm Gwen Kane. Devon's mom."

He was speechless. Devon's mom? This was the woman who caused Devon's abandonment issues?

"I heard you've been protecting Devon ever since Robert died. When I heard you two were in Atlanta, I did everything I could to try and find you and make sure Devon was all right. I was the one who followed you the night you left the hospital."

Reese started. "That was you?"

She shrugged sheepishly. "I thought I was good at tailing a car, but I guess you're even better at losing a tail. But the night Keith was killed, I followed you home again, and this time, you didn't notice me."

Reese found his voice through his shock. "What's going on?"

"I need you to get your gun and come with me. I'll explain on the way."

"On the way to where?"

"To get Devon," she said, and her next words confirmed his fears. "She's still in danger."

CHAPTER FORTY-FOUR

While Daphne had been awfully chatty in the bar, once she'd helped me into the passenger seat of the car and started to drive me back to the condo I was renting, she'd gone eerily quiet.

"I want to thank you for everything you've done," I said, slightly slurring my words. "I can see why my father depended on you so much. He spoke very highly of you, and I'd like you to continue on as my assistant."

Daphne remained silent, her eyes fixed on the road ahead.

"Are you all right?" I asked.

"I'm great," she said, looking over at me, smiling. "That's very generous of you. Thank you."

"I'm going to change this whole company around, and I want you to be there to help me."

She looked over at me for a moment longer and then returned her focus to the road, but not before I realized that her eyes were clear and alert, whereas I suddenly felt drowsy, and my tongue felt heavy. Did she drink anything at all? Of course she did because I saw the two glasses of tequila she ordered.

I turned my head to the side and closed my eyes, and then I heard Daphne murmur something that I didn't quite catch. I tried to lift my head from the headrest, but it wasn't cooperating.

"Did you say something?"

"It wasn't supposed to end like this," she said, softly.

"What do you mean?"

"Robert was supposed to tell you. We were going to tell you together and make plans on how to proceed. But the son of a bitch just had to die before saying anything, or at the very least, revising his Will."

My ears registered what she was saying, but my mind was so clouded with alcohol that I couldn't process it fast enough.

"His Will?" I asked. "Why would he revise his Will? I'm the sole heir."

Daphne turned toward me, her eyes now filled with anger. "You're not supposed to be the sole heir. I'm as entitled to that fortune and that company just as much as you are! In fact, I have even *more* of a right to it than you."

"What…what are you talking about?"

She laughed bitterly. "Isn't it usually the eldest child who's next in line to run the company?"

My breathing was becoming shallow, but I couldn't tell if it was from my drunken state or the bombshell she'd just revealed.

"I'm your sister, Devon. Robert was my father, too. He had an affair with my mother for years, but she never wanted to marry him. She was content in just being his mistress and reaping the financial benefits without having to take care of him as a wife. I was the result of their affair, and two years later, he had a baby with his wife, Gwen, and you, his legitimate child, was the apple of his eye."

My eyes were beginning to droop. I wanted so badly to go to sleep, but I had to stay alert. I had to hear what she was saying. Then realization smacked me in the face. This wasn't the effects of alcohol I was feeling. I'd been drugged.

"But even though I was a secret love child, Robert paid for my education and hired me on as his assistant at Foxworth Pharmaceuticals," Daphne continued. "I think it was his idea of a consolation prize, since you were the only daughter he claimed in public, and I had to remain a secret."

"But in recent years, I think the guilt finally got to him, because he began to promise me that he would tell you about me, and that I would take on a leadership role in the company. I held him to that promise, but I felt like he was stringing me along. He was reneging, so I had to take matters into my own hands."

"You sent the hitmen to my house to kill me that night," I said.

Her look turned regretful. "Sorry about that, but with you out of the way, he would have no choice but to leave the company to me. The company that was rightfully mine!"

"I knew all about his corrupt practices and the DEA closing in. He was going to prison, and I couldn't wait. Once the both of you were out of the way, I'd go to the board with my birth certificate and threaten to hand them all over to the DEA for corruption if they didn't vote me in as president and CEO. Once my title was secured, I'd change my last name to Foxworth. It should've been my name all along."

"Daphne, what are you going to do?" I slurred. "Where are we going?"

"To finish what those incompetent cops couldn't do."

I knew what that meant, and fear began to envelop me as I felt myself losing consciousness. "You...you don't have to do this."

"I'm sorry, little sister, but yes, I do."

I felt the car slow to a stop. I pried open my eyes and saw that we were at the entrance gate to the condos. She grabbed the key card from my purse and put it against the reader. The gates swung open, and she drove a short distance until she came to the private garage of my condo. The garage door slowly opened, and she pulled inside. She left the car running as she leaned over and undid my seatbelt. I tried to muster every last bit of strength to swat her in the eyes, but my arms felt like jelly.

"Sshh," she said, and spoke so soothingly. "All you need to do is just close your eyes and go to sleep. It'll be painless, I promise. Just go to sleep."

I gazed at her through heavy lids that were nearly closed to slits, and I could almost see the compassion she felt looking back at me.

"I'm sorry, Dev," she said. "If only Dad had kept his promises."

With that, she got out of the car, closed the door, and the next sound I heard was the garage door closing, trapping me inside with the car engine still running.

CHAPTER FORTY-FIVE

The brakes squealed as Reese brought the car to an abrupt stop at the front entrance of the condos where Devon was staying. Just as he and Gwen got out of the car, they saw Daphne striding out of the side gate.

"Stop right there!" Reese commanded, pulling his gun out and aiming it at her.

Daphne halted. "Reese! What—what are you doing here?"

"Where is she?"

"What are you doing?" Daphne asked, alarm filling her voice as she raised her hands.

"Where is Devon?" Reese asked.

"I don't know. I called and texted her to see if she needed anything from me tonight, but she never responded. I got worried, called an Uber, and came to see her. I just left her condo, but no one answered the door. I'm sure she just went to bed early. It's been an exciting day."

"That's a damn lie! Where's my daughter?" Gwen asked, getting out of the car.

"Gwen, let me handle this," Reese said, still keeping his eyes on Daphne.

He saw Daphne's eyes shoot over to Gwen, and the alarm and feigned surprise covering her face slowly melted away and morphed into scorn.

"My goodness, it's the infamous Gwendolyn." Daphne laughed. "You really did a number on little Devon when you left. Do you know that you're the reason Robert always coddled her? That spoiled little bitch is so afraid everyone she loves is going to leave her like you did that she has to hold onto them and control them like a puppet master."

"Just tell me where she is," Gwen pleaded.

Daphne cocked her head to the side and made a sad face. She then turned her attention on Reese. "Okay, you got me, but this is partly your fault, you know? All you had to do was hand her over to Vick and Jones. I would've given you the records from your daughter's clinical trials, and this would've been over weeks ago."

"There are no files," he said.

"Yes, there are," she insisted. "And I can still get them for you. But first, do me one small favor." She paused and looked to Gwen. "Shoot her."

"How can you be so heartless?" Gwen asked.

"Shoot her," Daphne commanded, ignoring Gwen. "Don't let her continue to stand here knowing her daughter is slowly dying."

Slowly dying? Fear gripped Reese's heart like a vice.

He cocked his gun and kept a steady aim at her heart. "Where's Devon? I'm not going to ask again."

"You're not going to shoot me, Reese," Daphne said, her voice too calm. "I can understand you shooting Jones. Good riddance to both of those incompetent fools, but you're not going to kill me, because I know where Devon is."

She was right. He couldn't kill her, but instinct told him Daphne was stalling with all this talking she was doing. And if she was stalling, that meant Devon was still somewhere close by and alive.

He moved in and kept his gun on her as he frisked her. He found a set of keys in her left pants pocket and tossed them to Gwen.

"Check the condo," he said. "She may still be there. And call the police."

As Gwen hurried away, Reese turned Daphne back in the direction from where she'd been coming from and pushed the gun into her back.

"Walk," he ordered, but with every minute that passed, he felt that Devon was running out of time.

He started to call her name over and over, hoping that wherever she was, she could still hear the sound of his voice.

"Devon!"

* * *

I tried to reach over and turn the ignition, but my hands were now immobile at this point. I could hardly move my fingers. Warm tears spilled over onto my cheeks as I thought about my mother and how harshly I'd spoken to her. I should've said I'd missed her. I should've made plans to meet with her for lunch so we could talk about everything. Now the last words she'd hear from me was *I don't want to see you.* I let those thoughts go and tried to search my mind for something more comforting. So I thought of Reese and how we'd made love again after all these years, and how explosive it had been. Yes, as darkness surrounded me, I'd just keep thinking of him.

My imagination was stronger than I'd believed because I could swear I heard him calling my name.

"Devon!"

"Yes," I called back, softly, still believing it was all in my head. "I'm here."

"Devon!"

The sound of his voice was slowly breaking through the haze, and I realized I wasn't imagining him. Reese was somewhere on the other side of the garage, calling for me.

"Devon!"

I couldn't move, but my voice still worked, so I gathered what little remaining strength was left in me, opened my mouth, and released a blood-curdling scream. I screamed for my life.

CHAPTER FORTY-SIX

"Your father was a brilliant man," my mom said, "but he had one big vice, and that was his wandering eye. For a long time, I chose to put up with all the women, because not only was he brilliant at his work, he was also a very good father."

I lay in the hospital bed, breathing in oxygen and listening to her retell the past.

"But there came a time where I couldn't turn a blind eye to it anymore, especially when one of those affairs resulted in a child. So, one day while he was at work, I packed my things and your things and moved us into an apartment I'd rented without him knowing. I left the divorce papers on a table by the door where he'd see them."

I closed my eyes, thinking back to a time where I remembered her telling me we were going on an adventure. I was excited about being in a cab and the ride across town to a place I'd never been. When we got to the apartment, she put me in my own room with the few toys she'd brought with us and told me to play by myself while she got dinner ready. But dinner never came. The next thing I remembered, my dad came into my new room, picked me up, and told me we were going back home.

"What happened?" I asked.

"Robert found out where we were. We had a big argument and he told me that if I wanted to divorce him, so be it. But I wasn't going to take you with me. He said if I tried to pursue custody of you, even shared custody, he would use his money and influence to prove me an unfit mother, and I'd never see you again."

"But you never did see me again."

"I'd see you at your school during recess. I was at every graduation from elementary all the way through college. I was even at your wedding—both of your weddings. I was just never allowed to speak to you. That was the agreement. He kept me on the board and allowed me to walk away with shares of the company, but that was my only consolation. No woman has ever left Robert, and because I dared to do it, he wanted to see me punished for it, and the best way to punish me was through my child."

I closed my eyes to more details about my father that I wasn't yet ready to face. He'd said it himself in his letter: I would hear things about him that would disappoint me.

"You said you were there during my college years and at my wedding," I said. "I was a legal adult by then. Dad may have had power over me as a minor, but when I turned eighteen, you could've come to me. You were free to see me as much as you wanted."

She shook her head sadly. "I know, but too much time had passed, and I feared all the lies he must've told you about me. I know he had to have told you I left you without a care, and I was scared what would happen if I came back into your life after so many years without you."

"How did you know about Daphne?" I asked.

"There had been something very familiar about her," my

mom said. "I had only seen pictures of her when she was just a child. After my bitter divorce from Robert and the threats he made against me, I chose to wash my hands of the whole thing. I was only interested in keeping up with you and being forced to watch you grow up from afar. But when I saw Daphne, all these years later, something told me I knew her, and I couldn't shake the feeling that something was wrong."

"She said she and Dad were going to introduce her to me as my half-sister, but I think she wanted to take over more than build a relationship with me," I said, looking down at the IV in my arm and trying to assimilate the questions I would never get answers to.

My mom reached over and clutched my hand. "I'm sorry for everything you went through. After I'd heard Robert was killed, I tried my best to find you. I finally called Michaela, and she told me what was happening. But I had no idea Daphne was trying to kill you, and I should've been there to stop her."

Tears began to slowly stream freely down my cheeks, and I looked up at her, reacquainting myself with her face. As a child, she was the most beautiful, kind, and gentle person I knew, and I wanted so much to tell her that and to make up for the past. That would all come in time. But for now, I simply squeezed her hand back, content with the fact that she was once again, in my life.

CHAPTER FORTY-SEVEN

wo weeks later
"Thank you all for coming. It has been a very diffi-cult month for my family and my business, and I appreciate your patience while my team and I work to sort it all out. However, I want you all to know that I have given my full cooperation to the DEA, the CBI, the APD, and all other law enforcement agencies until the investigations involving my father, Robert Foxworth, my late husband, Terrence Miller, and my...my sister, Daphne Coles have been resolved.

"I'm embarrassed, ashamed, and devastated by my father's actions. Our company has made many mistakes. Grave errors that may have cost lives, and I am assuming all responsibility for those mistakes.

"From this day forward, I'm committed to providing new lead-ership and doing what it takes to move this company forward in a positive direction."

"Ms. Foxworth?"

I tapped a key on my laptop, pausing the replay of my press conference from this morning, and gave my attention to my new assistant.

"Mr. Hunter is here to see you."

"Thank you, Zoey. You can send him in," I said, and rose from my desk, which was covered with piles of memos and documents that I had yet to give my full attention.

I came around to the front of the desk, smoothing imaginary wrinkles down the front of my white Ralph Lauren knee-length pencil dress. I then started to fluff out the waves of my hair before I told myself to stop. I put my hand down just as Reese strode in, looking both casual and breathtaking in dark blue jeans and a crisp white dress shirt with one button undone.

"Hi. I got your text," he said.

"Thank you for coming," I said, stepping toward him. "Can I get you something to drink?"

He raised a hand as a silent refusal and looked around the office that I had repainted in natural earth tones with new furnishings and artwork to match.

"You moved into your father's office," he said. "And you redecorated. The last time I was in here, it didn't look this cheerful."

I smiled, also looking around. "Yeah. I thought maybe I should have just repurposed another office for myself, but—"

"But it's your company now, and you deserve the big office."

My smile grew wider. "I do, don't I?"

"That's why he gave you everything you needed to start over."

"That's what I still don't understand," I said, leaning against the front of my desk. "If I was carrying the proof on my wrist this whole time, why did he give me a passkey to his office? I could've accessed those files from anywhere."

Reese thought for a moment. "All right, look. Robert may have been a liar, a thief, corrupt—"

"I get it."

"—But for all his faults, he was a good father, and no one could deny he loved you. Maybe the passkey was just a symbol that he always wanted you to take over. Years ago, you told me you talked to him about the changes you wanted to make in the company, the changes you're making now, and you thought he was just pretending to be interested and not really taking you seriously. But he did take you seriously, and he really was listening."

It was like my father was two different men, but Reese's words gave me some comfort, knowing the man I looked up to for years wasn't always a villain.

"Thanks," I said with a smile. "I needed to hear that."

"No problem."

We stood there smiling and observing each other for a short while, until he looked down at his watch.

"I'm kind of on a tight schedule, so what did you want to see me about?"

My breath caught. "Am I keeping you from something?"

"I'm heading back to San Francisco, and my plane leaves in two hours."

"Why?" I asked, not at all meaning to blurt out the first thing that came to my mind.

He chuckled. "My business here is done. I've given the authorities my statement, and I can officially say you're no longer in any danger. Also, I kind of need to get back to my business, my home, and my dog."

"Oh. Oh, of course," I said, quickly regaining my composure. "I just wanted to thank you, I mean genuinely thank you, for saving my life."

"My pleasure."

"I also wanted you to know that I'm working with the DEA to ensure they have everything they need to close the case against my father. I sent a formal statement to the CBI telling them what I witnessed in Agent Landon's death. Most of all, I wanted you to know I'm cleaning house completely here. I'm giving the company a new name and a new mission. We're moving away from prescription medication to build wellness spas, holistic treatment centers, and fund research for alternative medicines."

I paused and looked him squarely in the eye. "And I'm going to need someone with your skills to help me with all of that."

He tucked his hands in his jeans pockets and rocked back on his heels. "Devon—"

"Let me finish. I'm not offering you the vice-president position, but I would like you to be my Chief Technology Officer. It'll be the same as running your investigations firm. I'll give you full license over the cyber division, and you'll make more with me than the FBI pays you. It's just my way of thanking you, not just for keeping me safe, but for all of this." I paused to raise my arms and gesture around the office. "You convinced me that I was good enough to run this place. Somewhere deep down, I believed it myself, but I was always happy to let my dad, Terrence or some other man run the show."

He stepped forward and placed his hands to the sides of my face, bent his head forward and kissed me so lightly, it made me crave more. He kissed me on the lips once more, the sides of my face, and finally my forehead before dropping his hands and stepping away.

"I'm going to miss you," he said.

I moved away from him, my face twisting into a frown. "So you're turning me down?"

"Not you. Just the job."

My ego refused to believe that. I felt that, once again, he was rejecting me. He was walking out on me. Of all the men I'd ever wanted, he was the only one I could never seduce, tempt, manipulate, or just agree to do what I wanted him to do. And because of that, he was the only man I truly ever loved, and it angered me.

He must have seen the anger blanketing my face because he sighed heavily.

"Let's not leave it like this."

"How should we leave it?" I asked, my voice dripping with sarcasm. "Was I really the only one in this situation stupid enough to think we might have a chance to—I don't know—make up for lost time?"

"No, I thought about it. Many times."

"And?"

"And I saw that it couldn't work."

His brutally honest words paralyzed me.

"Why?" I asked. "Why are you walking away now?"

"Because you still want to keep me chained to you."

"No, I don't!"

"This job you're offering isn't for me, it's for you. You lost your dad and your husband, and now you need to find a way to keep me. So, what do you do? You toss money at me, just like you used to." He threw up his hands as frustration erupted from him. "Goddammit, Devon, do you really think your wealth is the only reason a man would want to be with you? You really believe that's all you have to offer? You are so much more than that fucking money!"

I laughed bitterly. "Well, fine then, I won't pay you. Will that make you happy?"

"No, what will make me happy is when you finally get over the fear of people leaving you."

"But it's not just any random people leaving me, Reese," I said, raising my voice. "It's the people I love who leave me. My dad, my mom, Terrence, and now you. You're leaving me! Again!"

A knock sounded at the door and Zoey cautiously peeped

her head inside. "I'm sorry to disturb, Ms. Foxworth, but is everything okay?"

"We're fine, Zoey. I'm sorry for the disturbance."

"Yes, ma'am," she said, and slowly closed the double doors.

"Devon—" he began.

"I'm sorry for my outburst. Just forget I said anything, all right? You're right. You have a business, a life, and other responsibilities in San Francisco. It was selfish of me to ask you to leave all that behind."

Reese looked as if he wanted to continue the conversation, but I was done. I'd just admitted out loud that I loved him when I hadn't meant to do that, and when he hadn't said he loved me. I needed this conversation to be over.

"It was a very generous offer," he said.

I nodded.

"I'm sure you'll have no trouble finding a good candidate."

He was trying to soothe my ego, which only fueled my anger.

"Despite what I said, I'm not going to fall apart if you're not around," I said.

"I know you won't. You're a strong, capable, and brilliant woman."

"And it's not as if we're in a relationship," I added.

His eyes were laser focused on me, and his expression didn't change. "That's right."

"So, whether you leave or not, just know it doesn't bother me."

"Then why are you crying?"

I swiped one side of my face with the back of my hand and sure enough, it came away wet with tears. Damn.

I abruptly turned around to my desk, grabbed something from it, and placed it into the palm of his hand. He looked down and saw it was a USB key.

"It's what you've been searching for all along. In those digital files my dad left me, there were other confidential files, including the ones from the drug trials. I made a copy for you. Everything you need to prove negligence is in there. Consider it payment for keeping me safe."

He looked down at the USB key and then up at me and tried again. "Don't end things like this."

"You have a plane to catch, Reese."

He continued to stare at me, but I refused to make myself any more vulnerable to him. Finally, he turned away, and when his back was to me, I could for just a moment drop the mask and let the pain wash over my face. But at the door to the office, he put his hand to the handle and then suddenly turned around.

"By the way, I saw your press conference this morning."

I fixed my face to a mask of indifference once again and tilted my head up. "Let me guess, you thought I was full of shit."

He slowly shook his head. "No. Like always, I thought you were amazing."

He then turned, opened the door, and closed it behind him. The sound carried among the four walls of the spacious office like an echo, reminding me all over again that even being amazing wasn't enough to hold onto the man I desired.

CHAPTER FORTY-EIGHT

Reese dragged himself into his apartment, dropped his carry-on at his feet, and knelt to greet Emma, who padded over to welcome him home.

"Did you miss me, girl? I missed you, too," he said, rubbing behind her ears.

He heard movement and looked up to see Teresa clutching a small duffel bag.

"I wanted to wait until you got back," she said, and handed him a key.

"What's this?" he asked, rising to his feet.

"What does it look like? It's the key to your place."

He took the key in his hand and frowned. "Why are you giving this to me?"

"Because I don't think our little arrangement is going to work anymore."

He rolled his eyes and sighed. "If this is about the story, I'm sorry. I changed my mind."

"No, it's not about the story, and even if it was, I wouldn't be angry with you about that. I'm glad you dropped it. It wasn't helping you at all in healing from Bella's death.

Besides, I have a better story. A certain heiress has given me exclusive rights to tell her harrowing adventure about escaping hitmen and revamping her corrupt company."

Reese smiled. "She's letting you tell her story?"

Teresa's face beamed. "Damn right, and my editor is giving me an assistant to help me with the research."

He gestured to the key in his palm. "So what does that have to do with this?"

"Because, whether you want to admit it or not, there's still something between you two, and as casual as our little thing was, I think it best we stick to just being friends."

Reese shrugged with nonchalance, not wanting to admit she was right. Even though he and Devon weren't together, something had been reignited in him while she'd been here, and it would be a long time before he could get her out of his mind again. That is, if he ever did get her out of his mind.

"So I take it that since you're not rushing by me to reserve a U-Haul or calling your partners to discuss selling them your part of the business that things didn't end in happily ever after in Atlanta."

He groaned. "Christ, not you, too."

"What?" she asked. "Come on Reese, you can't tell me you didn't think about what would happen between you two after this was all over."

"She said the same thing, and yeah, I thought about it. But I also let it go because I knew it wouldn't work."

"And how do you know that? You haven't even given it a chance. Just like—"

"Just like last time, I know!"

He stalked by her, headed to the kitchen, and grabbed a bottle of water from the fridge. He took a long swig and then pounded the bottle onto the counter. He then gripped the edge and shook his head in wonder at how much of a complete idiot he was.

"For so long, I convinced myself that she had abandonment issues, and yes, she does. She legitimately has fears of people leaving her and that's why she tries to keep a tight leash. But, for the first time in ten years, we're both single and free to be with each other, and I chose to walk away, again."

He left the rest unsaid, the part that was glaringly obvious—that *he* was the one who was really afraid. That after his daughter died, he was scared to death of opening his heart and letting someone else inside for fear he'd lose them.

Teresa rounded the counter, put her hand to his back, and rubbed it sympathetically.

"Call me a romantic, but maybe you two really need each other. Maybe together, you can help each other get over those fears. You understand each other."

He scoffed. "Yeah, two neurotic people in love."

Teresa laughed. "Yeah. Like the rest of the world."

CHAPTER FORTY-NINE

"She's in there," James said.

When I saw him leaving Michaela's hospital room, I braced myself for a tongue-lashing. The last time we had seen each other, he was warning me to leave his wife alone. Now he was telling me to take my time with her while he went to the cafeteria for a coffee break.

"Thanks," I said.

"Devon, hold on a minute."

I started to open the room door and then let it go. I turned back to look at him. James glanced around the semi-busy hallway at the nurses, doctors and other hospital staff who walked by and then stepped closer to me.

"I owe you an apology for the way I spoke to you. I know you love Michaela and would never purposely do anything to put her in danger. That night I found her beaten, I felt helpless seeing her like that and all I could think about was blaming you. Reese was right that none of this was ever your fault, and I was wrong for everything I said."

I took his hand in mine and clutched it. "I get it, James. I really do."

"You two are so different, but still so close, and I guess I never understood your friendship." He paused a moment before continuing. "But maybe I'm not supposed to get it. I'll just be happy you two have each other to count on."

I smiled, leaned forward, and kissed his cheek. "I love her and everything about her, and that includes you and the boys."

He nodded and gestured for me to go. "She's been asking for you."

I went inside, and when I saw Michaela, sitting up in bed with the oxygen tube gone and her bruises just beginning to heal, I took her into my arms and hugged her for a long time.

"Sit down," she said, her voice no longer raspy. "I've been dying over here not knowing if you're okay, and have only been able to get my information from the news."

I sat down in one of the chairs reserved for visitors, and for the first hour, I told her all about my board meeting, Daphne trying to kill me, how she was my half-sister, and how Reese and my mom had saved me.

"My God, that's so insane," she said, putting a hand to her chest. "Your life is a freaking soap opera!"

We shared a laugh.

"So, you and your mom are talking?"

I nodded. "Things are coming along with us. We're meeting for dinner tonight. I just don't know how to get over the fact that my dad led me to believe for years that she just left us—left me—without a backwards glance. How could he be so vindictive?"

"It sounds like he was hurt by her leaving him," Michaela suggested. "Either that, or his ego was bruised."

I shook my head. "Knowing my dad, it was definitely his ego."

"You've got to find a way to let it all go," she said. "He's not here anymore to answer the millions of questions you have for him. You need to find a way to heal and move on. But just know you have me, and you have your mom to help you."

I smiled. "I know."

"Okay, enough mushy stuff," she said, readjusting herself to sit up straighter in the bed. "Now, how's business?"

"Business is good," I said, reaching behind her back to fluff and adjust the pillows. "We broke ground on the first wellness spa, and I already found a site for the research center. I've been in meetings with contractors all week."

"Well, I'll be discharged tomorrow, and then I can start implementing these plans I've started designing for the wellness spa."

"I love that we're working together," I said, beaming.

Michaela shared my smile and then waited a beat. "Is it all right if I ask?"

"No need. He's back in San Francisco," I said, guessing her question. "I offered him a job, and he turned me down flat."

Michaela's eyes flooded with sympathy.

I shrugged. "It was a stupid fantasy. What did I expect? For him to magically fall in love with me after spending only a few weeks together? We only dated for months before we almost got married, and he wasn't in love with me even then."

"Stop it! That's not true. Reese was so in love with you. I could see it. We all saw it. He regrets every day not showing up to marry you. Why can't you believe that?"

"Because the way I treated him years ago, and the way I treated him now, I wouldn't show up for me, either."

"Devon," she said, sadly.

"It's true," I said, "and I don't care, because I'm done feeling sorry for myself." I gestured to her sketchbook. "Show me the designs for the spa."

Michaela continued to look at me sympathetically, but I

returned her stare with eyes that silently pleaded with her to drop the subject of Reese.

"Please, Michaela."

She held out for a moment longer and then gestured for me to climb into the bed with her. I eagerly slipped off my heels, removed my fitted blazer, and carefully climbed into the double bed next to her. She scooted over and grabbed her sketchbook while I lay my head on her shoulder as together, we swooned and gushed over her designs.

CHAPTER FIFTY

One month later

Once I thanked the last of the well-wishers for their condolences and kissed my mother goodbye, promising her that we'd meet for lunch next week, and then hugged Michaela and James, I gratefully allowed my driver to escort me inside the black town car. Once the door was closed, I let go a sigh filled with so many emotions that were hard to name.

It was the second funeral I'd attended this month, and it was the most emotional one, because it was my father's. For Terrence's funeral, I allowed his mother and sisters to make the arrangements, and when all was said and done, I simply handed them my American Express card. I also made sure to meet with my estate lawyer and set up trust funds for Terrence's two nieces and his biological daughter, Kimberly Sawyer. Her parents, Havilland and Eric, who flew into town for the funeral, vehemently refused the trust, but I wouldn't hear of it. Terrence would have wanted it this way. Once he was laid to rest, I said a prayer and whispered to him that no matter how our marriage had been, I loved him because he was my husband.

For my father, a lot of mixed feelings came up. I loved him dearly for the love, kindness and generosity he showed me as a child and a woman, and I knew that I was incredibly lucky to have had a father like him. However, I didn't know how to feel about the part of him that was secrets, lies, and corruption. With my mother standing to one side and Michaela on my other side, I decided to simply forgive him and let those dark parts simply die with him.

I leaned my head back against the headrest as my driver maneuvered through the Atlanta streets. It was the first time in a long time that I was alone, and for once, being alone didn't frighten me. I welcomed the peace and tranquility.

Finally, we arrived at the gated community where I'd purchased a new house for myself. It wasn't a mansion at all, but a two-story, four-bedroom, brick colonial-style home complete with a wraparound porch, deck, and large back-yard. I pictured inviting my mom, Michaela, James, and their boys over for barbecues, and the image always made me smile.

My driver pulled the car into the driveway and got out to open the door for me. As soon as the car door swung open, I looked up to thank him and my breath caught at the sight of Reese standing there in a black suit and black tie.

"I called your office," he said, "but your assistant said you were booked for a month and that I needed to make an appointment to see you. I couldn't wait that long, so I followed you home."

I nodded my thanks to the driver, stepped out of the vehi-cle, and clutched my purse as I stood before him.

"You're supposed to be in California."

"I was, but I came back for your father's funeral."

I frowned. "You were at the funeral? I didn't see you there."

"I wasn't trying to be seen." He looked behind him at my house. "I really do need to talk to you. May I come in?"

After wishing the driver a good day, I walked up the porch steps to the house, feeling Reese's presence behind me.

"This is nice," he said. "But don't you own a mansion in Milton now?"

As much as I'd tried to resist, a smile still ghosted the corners my lips. "I own a lot of things now, but it doesn't mean I'm going to keep it all. Besides, it's just me. Why would I ever need all that space?"

We stepped into the sparse foyer, and I closed the door behind him. "I just moved in and the furniture hasn't been delivered yet, so there's really no place to sit."

"It's all right," he said, taking off his suit jacket and laying it across a chair by the door. "I'm here to see you, not to be entertained."

I shrugged. "I can't imagine what for. You already turned down my offer to stay with me and work with me."

He chuckled. "I turned down the offer to work for your company. I never said I didn't want to be with you."

I rolled my eyes. "Please, Reese. It's been a long day. Actually, it's been a long few months, and I'm not exactly in the right headspace for games."

His brow furrowed. "You think I'm here to play games?"

I started to turn away from him, but he gently grabbed my elbow and brought me back around to look at him. "Answer me."

I groaned. "You leave, you come back, you leave again, and you come back again. My life isn't a revolving door."

"You're right. But that's not what I'm doing. I came back because there are three things I need to say to you."

I gestured to my cell phone resting on a small table by the door.

"No need to waste money on a plane ticket."

"Yeah, but you gave back the burner phone, and I never asked for your new number. You have my number, but after a few weeks, I got the feeling you weren't going to call."

I almost did. As soon as I got a new cell phone, I plugged his number in, but each time I scrolled to his contact information and hovered my thumb over the phone icon, my courage failed me. What would I say? I miss you Reese? I love you Reese? I never stopped loving you Reese?

"It doesn't matter," he continued. "The first thing I want to say is that I'm not going through with the negligence suit. I'd decided that weeks ago, but when you gave me the proof I needed and publicly accepted responsibility for your father's actions, I knew I was going after the wrong person. I didn't want to damage you, especially when I heard you talk about all the changes you want to make to the company. I don't care what anyone told you in the past, you'll be a wonderful CEO, and your father knew that, too."

"Reese, you don't have to—"

"Just let me get this out," he said. "It was never about your father, the FDA, or even about revenge. I never really wanted revenge. I just wanted my little girl back."

With every word he spoke, I was growing dangerously close to letting my guard down. "I understand."

"The second thing is our wedding."

"You already apologized for that."

"I'm talking about afterward. Not showing up at our wedding was bad enough, but when you came looking for me that night, I never should've let you walk out that door. I've regretted that for years. I regretted it even more that day I came to see your father about Bella's treatment. You walked in his office, and for just a few seconds, I forgot how much pain I was in. You've always been able to do that for me."

"That's very sweet, Reese, but remember that you left because I was such a control freak," I reminded him. "I was afraid you'd leave me if I ever gave you too much freedom, so I had to control where you worked and where we lived. I couldn't even let you buy my wedding ring. I tried the same control tactics with Terrence, and it backfired. I probably would've ruined us, too."

"Whether we would've lasted or not, I should've given us the chance to find out."

He paused and put his hands on my shoulders.

"No matter how much you tried to take control of every situation, you were always loving and compassionate. When Bella was sick, I wanted to reach out to you, but I thought, how could I possibly ask you for comfort when I'd left you in so much pain?"

I held back the tears that threatened and cleared my throat. "I'm sure you were a wonderful father. Bella was loved, and you deserve love, too."

I closed the distance between us, wrapping my arms around his neck, and he wrapped his arms around my waist. Together, we stood there holding each other, breathing into one another and soaking up the loss he felt between us.

He then pulled away from me. "Well, that's all I wanted to say. I really do hope we can keep in touch. Despite everything you went through, it really was a pleasure having you in my life again, if only for a short time."

I wanted so much to throw myself into his arms again and never let him go, but I'd been rejected by him too many times to take that risk again. So, I simply nodded.

"Sure. I'd like that, but I thought there were three things you wanted to say. What was the third?"

He rubbed the back of his head. "Yeah, I guess it was just two."

We didn't say anything more as he turned and headed for the front door. I followed behind him, watching as he grabbed his suit jacket from the chair and slung it over his shoulder. He then looked around the house once more.

"This really is a nice place. It suits you much better than that big, empty—"

His words stopped abruptly, and I noticed as he was looking around, his gaze had swung to the left. My home office was that way, and when I followed his eyes, I realized what he must have seen. I closed my eyes and shook my head, silently chastising myself for not closing the office door before leaving for the funeral that morning. In a rush of panic, I searched my mind for a distraction.

"So, what time is your flight? I can call my driver back and have him take you to the airport. Atlanta traffic at this time of day—"

He put up a hand to stop me and walked toward my office. I slowly followed after him, my high heels echoing along the wood floor as we walked the short corridor. The double French doors were open and the large artist's rendering on cardboard stock was displayed on an easel in the middle of the room. I watched Reese as he looked over the rendering, and then I turned to the picture and admired the glass building surrounded by lush green trees, shrubs, and pink hydrangeas.

The Bella Hunter Cancer Research Center.

Silence filled the room for a long while before Reese slowly turned from the picture and faced me.

"I didn't mean for you to see that right now," I said. "We just closed on the site and we're still gathering plans and talking to contractors. I wanted to show it to you after—"

Reese stopped me again, this time by abruptly snaking his

hand around my waist, and pulling me into him. In the next instant, his lips were on mine, stealing my breath. He explored me, tasted me, and claimed me. I couldn't hold back the pleasurable moan and wrapped my arms around his neck to deepen the kiss. I relished his touch as our bodies molded together. I needed this so much after weeks of nothing but stress.

I needed Reese.

The kiss slowed and then stopped, but he didn't pull away from me, and instead put his forehead to mine and spoke in a whisper.

"I love you. I love you so much."

I looked up at him. "You do?"

"That was the third thing, but I lost my nerve, and I was about to be a fucking idiot again and walk out of here without telling you."

He kissed me again. "I love you, Devon. I always have."

Finally, I let the tears fall.

"I love you, too. That day I saw you in my father's office, I wanted so much to go after you and see that you were all right. But my anger and old memories still had the better of me."

"Yeah, me too." He brushed strands of my hair away from my face and our gazes clashed. "It's way past time for new memories."

He tossed his jacket to the side, bent low at the knees, and slowly raised my skirts until his palms were gripping my ass in the black lace panties I was wearing. He then lifted me and planted me onto my desk. I tugged off his tie, tossed it across the room, and we fought at unbuttoning his shirt. He moved his hands to my back and unzipped my dress, letting it fall past my shoulders to the black lace bra I wore underneath. He slipped one bra strap down, softly kissed my shoulder, and then his lips moved lower to the curve of my breasts. He latched his mouth onto one of my nipples and flicked his tongue rapidly against it. Fireworks exploded in my head as I clutched at him, spread my legs wide, and rubbed against the hardness behind his trousers.

With my dress hiked up around my waist, I shoved papers off my desk and leaned back. Reese followed me, leaning over to cover my body while unzipping his trousers and then dipping his fingers low to move aside my panties.

I sucked in a breath, anticipating the moment when I would feel the length of him gliding into me, and I didn't have to wait long. The moment I felt him filling me, I wrapped my legs around him. With my shoes still on, I crossed my feet at the ankles, locking Reese into me. For this sensual moment, he indulged my fears by letting me keep him close to me.

"You're not going anywhere," I moaned as he moved in and out of me.

"No, I'm not," he grunted.

"You're all mine," I said, lifting my hips and letting him take me.

Reese bent low and kissed me while he continued to stroke in and out of my wetness. I felt myself going light-headed as I tried to hold off the impending orgasm, but he kept a firm grip on my thighs as he relentlessly took hold of me, and I had to give up the fight.

"You're all mine!" I screamed, unable to hold back the sea of pleasure washing over me.

His speed increased, and soon, he erupted with a roar of his own and collapsed on top of me. I moved my hands to the top of his head to play with his hair and kept my legs wrapped tight around him, unwilling to let him go. As I combed my fingers through his hair, listening to his breathing calm, it was then that I heard his quiet declaration.

"I always was."

EPILOGUE

*S*ix *months later*

"Is everything all right?" I asked, lying in bed with the phone to my ear and the TV on mute.

"Everything's good," Reese said. "So good that my business finished early and I'm on my way back tonight. I feel a little unwanted. They don't seem to need me as much out here anymore."

"That's because you trained them well. Now, your business here in Atlanta, that's another story."

Reese laughed. "Yeah, time for me to come back and show them who's boss."

I smiled, once again feeling grateful his partners had refused to buy him out of the investigative firm. Instead, they'd suggested expanding the business by opening operations in Atlanta. He had his hands so full here training all-new staff that he'd had to resign from his consultant position with the FBI. His full attention was on the business—and me.

"I'm catching a red-eye flight out tonight."

"Good, because Emma and I miss you," I said rubbing her black coat. Since the two of them moved in four months ago,

I'd learned that Reese didn't allow her in the bed. But whenever he travelled back to San Francisco on business, I bent the rules because she was such good company.

"Also, we have a few more pre-marital sessions."

"I'll be there," he said.

I fell silent.

"I'll be there, Devon. I promise," he reiterated, and I knew he was talking about more than just the counseling appointments.

"No, it's not that. And I'm not worried about the wedding, because I hired some mercenaries to follow you around that entire day and I have their word there will be dire consequences for you if you don't show."

"So what you're saying is I should cancel my getaway flight to Mexico," he joked.

"Unless I'm on that flight with you, then yes, I suggest you cancel it."

We shared a laugh, and then it slowly died as I was once again lost in my thoughts. The wedding would be much smaller and intimate this time around, but I couldn't help but think about the one person who wouldn't be there.

"You're thinking about your father," he correctly assumed.

"It'll be weird without him there to walk me down the aisle. But I have my mom to do that, and somehow her walking me down the aisle to marry you feels like the way it should be."

More silence fell, but this time it was comforting and filled with all the love we felt for each other.

"Are you looking at it again?" Reese asked after a moment.

I put my left hand down and laughed. "I can't stop looking at it. It's beautiful."

"You're sure you like it? It's not the Tiffany ring you bought yourself ten years ago, but I can get you something very close to it. I make pretty good money now."

"Reese, stop. I love it, and I already told you I don't care about some silly ring. I just want to marry you."

He chuckled. "Do you still have it?"

"Um, yeah, it's somewhere around here. I haven't thought about it in years."

"All right, my Uber is here. I won't call when I land. It will be too early. Just be prepared for me to wake you."

I smiled with wicked anticipation. "Safe flight. I love you."

"I love you, too," he said, and ended the call.

I put the phone down, rose from the bed, and strode into the large walk-in closet and straight to the dresser where I kept my accessories and jewelry boxes. I pulled open a drawer to one case, and resting inside was a small ring box with the signature Tiffany blue-and-white ribbon. I gently untied it, removed the lid, and pulled out the ring box. I opened the lid, and nestled inside was a white gold ring with a three-carat solitaire diamond as its centerpiece. I smiled to myself as I pulled the ring out and admired its brilliance.

I looked down at Emma, who'd trailed after me into the closet and was now peering up at me.

"Don't judge me," I said to her, and then slowly brought the ring to my lips and kissed it.

* * *

Thank you for reading EXECUTION! If you enjoyed Reese and Devon's exciting love story, you'll love the explosive finale in the EX FILES series, EXTORTION.

The only way Drake Morgan can save his company is by marrying Cecily Reed. It was supposed to be a simple marriage of convenience, but the arrangement between them turns passionate...and deadly.

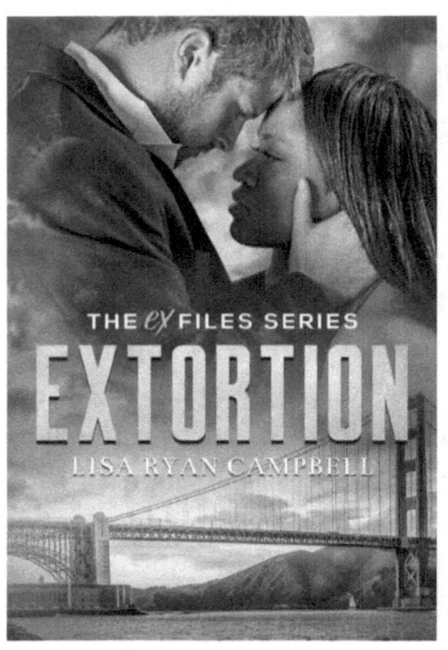

ONE-CLICK EXTORTION NOW >

"She has a talent of hooking you from the very beginning!"

"Excellent thriller!"

SIGN UP FOR LISA'S NEWSLETTER:

www.lisaryancampbell.com/newsletter

ABOUT THE AUTHOR

Award-winning Author, Lisa Ryan Campbell began writing as a small child using her mother's pink typewriting paper. Years later, she decided it was important to get a "real job" and attended Arizona State University to major in English with the goal of continuing on for both a Master's and Doctorate degrees in English and teach at the college level.

In 2002, Lisa graduated with a Bachelor's degree in English Literature and an Ancient Egyptian romance novel she wrote in her spare time. She decided then she would not be continuing on to graduate school, but instead joined Romance Writers of America and focused on her true love.

Lisa is an avid traveler and has seen many of the world's treasures in Egypt, Peru, Spain, France, Morocco, England, Mexico and the Caribbean. She spends her time mostly at her home in Colorado writing, reading and watching 1940's noir movies. She also loves to laugh, so you may frequently catch her watching reruns of Archer, Veep and The Office.

Sign up for Lisa's newsletter and find out more about her books at www.Lisaryancampbell.com and connect with her on social media.